THE LONG SILENT NIGHT

BY SHANE BERRYHILL

OTHERSIDE
PRESS

I jerk as I hear the intruder knocking around in the living room. He's making enough noise to awaken spring. Obviously, I'm not dealing with the brightest bulb on the Christmas tree here. I skate into the living room at full speed, flicking on strands of lights as I go. I yell, hoping to take him by surprise. "Get ready for a tall glass of justice—on the rocks!" I put on the brakes as I see that my oh-so-dangerous intruder is a polar bear cub—one that's probably wandered in looking for food. But it's too late. I spread my legs just in time to dodge Chilly Willy and I go crashing into the only greenery in the entire 'gloo—a Christmas tree.

The next thing I know, I'm lying on the floor with pine needles in places they have no business being and the cub licking my face. I sigh and pet the little guy. He barks happily in response. It's then the bells on the snow globe begin to jingle. I get to my feet, grimacing with pain as I yank pine needles out of my blue skin, and answer the globe.

"Frost, here."

"Oh, Jack!" Mom's image materializes in the globe's swirling snow. Not my real mom. I've never met her. But the mom that counts—the one who raised me like I was her own. She's upset. No, worse still, she's scared.

"What is it, Mom? What's wrong?"

"He's gone, Jack. Someone took him!"

"Who, Mom? Someone took who?"

There's a pause as mom gathers herself.

"Santa, Jack. Santa Claus has been kidnapped!"

Open this book and you will find the tale,
Of the long silent night, oft called the first noir-el.
It's a story of Jack Frost, the North Pole's private eye,
And the case of the missing jolly fat guy.

But it's not just about Christmas, you will soon see.
This book reads of all holidays throughout eternity.
Jack will visit the Emerald Isle and go Halloween side,
In search of his father and it will be one bumpy ride!

There will be action, adventure and a mystery for the ages,
For those brave enough to keep turning pages.
So turn off the tube and switch on your lamp light,
It's time to start reading THE LONG SILENT NIGHT.

CHAPTER 1

My eyes pop open and, despite the darkness and the eggnog pounding away in my head, it's clear as ice crystal that someone's in the igloo with me. I sit up in bed too quickly and the room spins. Got to lay off the 'nog.

I slip out of bed and make my way across the room, my bare blue feet gliding soundlessly over the frozen floor. I lean my back against the ice block wall and peek through the open doorway. Open because I don't have a bedroom door. This is the North Pole, after all. Land of candy canes and good will toward men. Who needs locked doors?

In truth, the Pole has its bad seeds just like everywhere else. Trust me. I know. And not just because I'm Jack Frost, private investigator—the Pole's one and only P.I., in fact.

I look into the pitch, but see nothing. If this little wake-up call is courtesy of the Old Man, by Great Ak's beard, I'm about to have a new ice sculpture in my living room!

I jerk as I hear the intruder knocking around in the living room. He's making enough noise to awaken spring. Obviously, I'm not dealing with the brightest bulb on the Christmas tree here.

I skate into the living room at full speed, flicking on strands of lights as I go. I yell, hoping to take him by surprise.

"Get ready for a tall glass of justice—on the rocks!"

I put on the brakes as I see that my oh-so-dangerous intruder is a polar bear cub—one that's probably wandered in looking for food. But it's too late. I spread my legs just in time to dodge Chilly Willy and I go crashing into the only greenery in the entire 'gloo—a Christmas tree.

The next thing I know, I'm lying on the floor with pine needles in places they have no business being and the cub licking my face.

I sigh and pet the little guy. He barks happily in response. It's then the bells on the snow globe begin to jingle. I get to my feet, grimacing with pain as I yank pine needles out of my blue skin, and answer the globe.

"Frost, here."

"Oh, Jack!" Mom's image materializes in the globe's swirling snow. Not my real Mom. I've never met her. But the Mom that counts—the one who raised me like I was her own. She's upset. No, worse still, she's scared.

"What is it, Mom? What's wrong?"

"He's gone, Jack. Someone took him!"

"Who, Mom? Someone took who?"

There's a pause as Mom gathers herself.

"Santa, Jack. Santa Claus has been kidnapped!"

Twas the night before Christmas, when at the North Pole,
Bad things were stirring as a storm began to blow.
All was not right in this snow-covered land.
Evil was afoot, working its diabolical plan!

Private Eye Jack Frost was asleep in his bed,
Last night's eggnog pounding in his head.
But despite Jack having a final nightcap,
His brain was razor sharp, just like a steel trap.

So when in his kitchen there arose such a clatter,
Jack sprang awake to see what was the matter.
He skated through his igloo, his feet sliding on ice,
To catch his home's invader and make him pay the price!

Jack slid into his kitchen and saw with his own eyes,
The intruder was a polar bear cub, much to his surprise!
Jack lost his balance and crashed to the floor,
His pride wounded, his ego bruised to the core.

The bear barked and gave Jack a lick.
Then the snow globe rang. It was the wife of St. Nick.
"Hi, Mom. What's up?" Jack said, then paused.
"Oh, Jack!" she replied. "They've kidnapped Santa Claus!"

CHAPTER 2

It's snowing hard when I arrive at the Bavarian fortress that is Christmas Castle. The blue-capped police elves have already zoned off the place with yellow tape. The trench-cloak and stocking-fedora I'm wearing allow me to go dim and slip by the blue caps guarding the front. Inside, there's more of the blue caps sweeping Holly-decked halls for evidence and questioning their better known cousins, the green-capped toy-makers.

I pass the den and see Alfie giving Mrs. Claus the third degree. Seeing the red-bearded little maniac grill my elderly, gray-haired mother gets my bells jingling big time! I start to intervene but catch a warning glance from Mom. Once upon a time, I baffled Pop with games of hide and seek, and he can see you sleeping, awake, whatever! But Mom, well, I could never hide from her.

I protest silently for a moment, but Mom casts an upward glance. That old broad—and I say that with only the greatest love and affection—doesn't miss a trick. I nod. She can handle Alfie. She's as smart and tough as they come. I know where she wants me—where I can do some good. I turn back down the hall and make my way up candy-cane-spindled stairs to the crime scene.

I enter Pop's bedroom and the expression "tarred and feathered" comes to mind. The large window that constitutes the eastern wall is shattered. Blustery, snow-laden winds rush inside, swirling the hundreds of dark feathers that blanket the room. Two blue caps jump around in front of me trying to gather the feathers into evidence bags.

I go visible so that I can snatch a feather from the air and examine it. Not that I couldn't do it while dim, if I had too. But being dim makes even the simplest of things seem like ice skating uphill backwards. Not that that would be hard for me, but you get the picture.

I snag one of the feathers and look it over. "Meleagris gallopavo," I whisper "*Turkey.*"

The blue caps immediately whirl on me, candy canes drawn and aimed at my chest. That's as high as they're able to point them. These are Christmas elves, after all, and *Legolas*, they ain't.

"Put your hands on your head and get down on the floor!" they say in unison.

"So you finally noticed I was in the room. Congratulations."

"Put your hands on your head and get down on the floor!" Blue Cap One says.

"Relax, boys. I'm one of the good guys. You know that."

"This is your last warning!"

"Oh, for Cringle's sake, Opie, I was a candle-bearer at your first Season's Greetings."

"We mean it, Frost!" Blue Cap Two says.

I give him a bit of the Eye.

"Don't give unless you're prepared to receive, Jangle!"

The *Eye*, or *Frosty Gaze* as it's normally called, is something I get from the Old Man—my real one. I've seen him literally freeze a person in their tracks with it, but the best I can do is send cold chills down someone's spine. It doesn't work on those with strong wills, but this time proves effective enough. Jangle gulps and takes a backward step.

"Frost!" Alfie's voice booms from behind me and suddenly my headache gets worse.

"Alfie, tell your boys to lose the sweets or it's about to get a lot colder in here!"

"Don't threaten me, Frost!" Alfie barks as he enters the room. He gestures for Opie and Jangle to holster their weapons. He's smarter than I thought. "I'll have you on ice so...that is...I mean...uh...how dare you waltz in here and contaminate my crime scene!"

"This 'crime scene' happens to be the castle I grew up in."

"So cry me an ice-flow! We all grew up here!"

"Boys," Mom says as she enters the room, another blue cap following at her considerably plump elbow.

"I'm sorry, Cap'," Blue Cap Three says, "I couldn't—"

"Oh holy night, Jingle!" Alfie yells. "This place is a circus! Bad enough we got this second-generation thug in here, but—!"

"Now, Alfie, you hush that up!" Mom scolds. "Jack is my son, and his heart is as good as yours or mine! You know better than to use that kind of language. You are supposed to be setting a good example for these fine young elflings!"

Alfie slumps his shoulders, defeated. "Yes, Mrs. Claus."

"That's better. Now, for your information, Jack's here because I asked him to come."

"You asked him?"

"That's right. And now I want the two of you to work together and figure out who's got my Santa!"

Mom's armor finally cracks and tears swell in her eyes and run down the rosy hills of her cheeks. I feel like I should be crying tears, too. But they'd only freeze before they left my eyes, so I don't.

"We will, Mom," I say as I pat her arm. The least I can do is fake sympathy, even if my heart is as cold as ice. "Now, why don't you go rest while Alfie and I talk?"

She nods and Alfie motions for the blue caps to escort her to her room so that we're left alone. I decide to overlook his earlier remarks about my being a thug and get down to business. It's Pop that's at stake here, after all. No point in wasting any more time fighting.

"Your boys find out anything from the green caps?" I ask.

"No one was seen entering or leaving the castle. But with the blizzard going on outside, you can't see two feet in front of your face."

"Any tracks?"

"The snow took care of that, too.

"So what do you think?"

"This is an obvious open and shut case. This is the Gobbler's work."

He gets frustrated when I don't answer. "Don't you think so?"

"Frankie certainly has motive," I say. "The Gobbler and his

crew have always been jealous of Pop. They've made no bones about being angry at people passing them over for Christmas the way they pass over the socks their great aunt puts under the tree for them."

"So you agree, then?"

"I think somebody certainly *wants* us to believe it's Frankie. But his entire flock would have had to waddle in here to leave behind this many feathers."

"What are you saying?"

"I'm saying this is a frame up. This crime scene has been staged."

"Nonsense! You said it yourself—Frankie's tired of getting the short end of the candy cane. Case closed!

"I agree you should have him picked up."

"Rudy and Yukon are already questioning him down at the station. They'll have Santa's whereabouts out of him in no time, not that there's any hurry."

"What do you mean there's no hurry? It's Christmas Eve. The kids are waiting."

Alfie shakes his head. "Santa had already conjured the night spell before he was hijacked."

"Night spell?"

"The spell of eternal night. It makes Christmas Eve last until every boy and girl in the world has received their Christmas presents."

"Call the spell off. Christmas can wait. It will have to."

"Ha! I hear what you're caroling, Frost, but Santa's the only one who can deck that hall. Without him, it's the long, silent night forever."

"Well, Merry Ho! Ho! Ho! And here I thought finding Santa and saving Christmas was all we had to worry about. Just holly jolly!"

My head feels like there's icebergs dancing inside it rather than sugar plums. I take off my stocking-fedora and massage my forehead.

"What does H-Town have to say about all this?" I ask.

"I didn't see any reason to involve the feds. The Pole is perfectly capable—"

"You've got to be twisting my tinsel, right?"

"Look, Frost," Alfie says, "despite what Mrs. Claus thinks, we blue caps are perfectly capable of finding Cringle without H-Town or some freezer burnt gangster reject skating around, sticking his pointy, icicled noise where it doesn't belong. You get me?"

"Wrapped with a bow and under the tree, Alfie."

"Good. I don't want to hear even a carol out of you until the Big C's back stuffing his jolly, fat face with cookies!"

"Merry Christmas to you, too, Alfie."

What an unholy night filled with fear.
No Santa, no sleigh, no tiny reindeer.
But do not worry; put on a happy face.
Private Eye Jack Frost is on the case!

With his concealing trench-cloak and stocking-hat,
Jack slipped past the Blue Caps in no time flat.
He made his way inside Santa's castle
Where he found his first clue, though it was a hassle.

Two blue capped elves ordered Jack to freeze,
Or his frosty person they would quickly seize.
Before they could, in came Captain Alfie.
He wasn't happy to see Jack, or listen to his mouthie!

"What do you want, Frost?" Alfie angrily asked,
For you see, he and Jack shared a troubled past.
"I'm here to help," Jack said, "in solving this crime.
"Whoever took Santa must have been paid quite a dime!"

"Frankie the Gobbler stole your pop," Alfie claimed,
"So Thanksgiving could have all of Christmas' fame!"
"No, no, no. Aren't we on the same page?
"Alfie, my friend, this crime scene has been staged!"

CHAPTER 3

Find him, Jack. Find your father. That's what Mom said to me before I left the castle. Oh, the irony.

The question here is, *who benefits?* That's what you've always got to ask yourself when working a case. Who benefits from Santa being out of the picture?

With the Awgwa monsters long vanquished, the question narrows down the list to, oh, about every holiday character in the known worlds, including the other versions of Cringle who'd like to raise their stock. With Santa out of the way, Christmas as we know it is a no-go and the icy tundra is wide open for any one of them to become the star at the top of the tree.

If I'm going to find Santa and fix this mess, then that list has to shrink. That's why I'm taking Mom's advice. I'm going to find my old man—*my real one.* Snow can't hit the fan like this on his turf without him knowing something about it. And something tells me it's no accident the snow's blowing like it is tonight.

It doesn't take long. I'm barely in the Outlands when I hear snow wolves barking in the distance. Soon, I spy a wolf-sled cresting the horizon with a dark figure at the reins, cracking a whip. Only one possibility there—*Bominable.* As in *the abominable snowman.*

In no time, he pulls alongside me. Half-man and half-polar bear, Bominable looks like a monster from your worst nightmare. He lifts a gigantic paw and cracks the whip over the heads of the sled-wolves. In truth, the wolves would've only slowed him down. He drove the sled for effect—to try to scare me. It works better than I care to admit.

"Jack," he says in a deep, gravelly voice as his smile reveals rows of yellow fangs.

I try to play it cool.

"All this for me, Bominable? I didn't know you were such a sweetheart. Next you'll be wearing plaid sweaters and sipping hot cocoa."

That throws him. His furry face curls into a snarl and a low growl issues from his gullet. I don't know whether I should be happy or jingling in my boots.

"Your father wants to see you."

I taunt him. It's the only weapon I've got against him. I mean, you ever try to freeze a snowman? A real one? It's as hard as you'd think! "Funny. And here I thought the Old Man was the one who left me alone down south that time to thaw."

"Character builder. He was trying to toughen you up."

"Oh yeah? Well what about—"

"I'm really enjoying this jaunt down memory lane, Jack, but I have my orders."

"You always were my old man's favorite trick dog, Bominable."

"Get on board, Frost. *Now.*"

"I'll skate on my own, thanks."

Bominable scowls. He'll be on thin ice with the Old Man for not following orders in full. But at the same time, he can't very well put the snowdrift on me since, technically, I'm the Old Man's son.

"I'll lead," I command him. "You follow."

He grunts, having little choice but to obey. But that doesn't stop Bominable from getting his licks in.

"The Old Man won't always be around to protect you, Frost. And with you wanting nothing to do with the family business, guess who's next in line for the job?"

"That's something you should think about. *Especially late at night when you're all alone in that cute little igloo of yours.*"

"Sticks and stones, Bominable," I say and then quickly turn around so he can't see my blue face turn white. The reaction has nothing to do with my headache.

We reach the mountain even faster than Bominable reached me. With the storm, I can't see the ice fortress at the peak, but

I know the Old Man's up there, peering down at me from his watchtower, the usual emotions of disappointment and disgust in his face.

The feeling's mutual, Old Man.

The mountainside is a sheer cliff of ice, rock, and snow. Insurmountable.

"Should we knock?" I ask.

Bominable smiles and chills run down my spine again as he reveals his fangs. At that moment, a gigantic, inverted tornado of swirling ice and snow drops out of the clouds and snakes its way downward. The earth shakes beneath our feet as it impacts the ground directly before us. When at last the tornado dissipates, an enormous ramp of frozen snow that climbs the entire length of mountainside is left behind. We stare at it for a moment, the silence of snow falling around us somehow foreboding in the wake of the twister's roar.

Bominable cracks his whip and sends the snow wolves scrambling up the newly created slope, breaking our trance. I skate after, building speed to get back in front. Sure, I'm on edge about seeing the Old Man, but I'll be thawed and cooked before I let him know it!

We reach the Old Man's medieval ice castle and it's so cold, even I want to shudder—but I don't. Bominable calls off the snowmen guarding the entrance. These snowmen aren't the furry kind like Bominable. They're the real deal. And like all the Old Man's soldiers, they bring new meaning to the lyrics 'Thumpity-thump-thump, look at Frosty go.' They scowl at me with their soulless coal eyes over their orange carrot beaks.

"Tough crowd." I mutter as we enter.

We pass giant icicle pillars and, if I didn't know better, what I'd think were the most life-like ice sculptures ever made. You don't want to make my father angry. Especially here in his own house.

We reach my father's throne room and Bominable bids me to wait in the hall. Even this deep in the fortress, I can hear the storm winds blowing outside. There will be a few more additions to my father's sculpture collection come morning. I pray I won't be one of them.

Bominable opens the door and goes in. Through the open door, I see a shuddering Eskimo bent over on one knee, kissing my father's ice ring in tribute and I'm six years old all over again, both sickened by and in awe of *Old Man Winter*.

Bominable reaches the Old Man and whispers in his ear. My father glances up at me through the open door and then shoos the Eskimo away. The native backs out of the room on his hands and knees. Bominable gestures for me to enter and I do.

Once upon a time, my father would've welcomed me with open arms. But those days are long gone. Now the Old Man eases back onto his throne to resume the formality and distance that must remain between king and subject.

His blue face, silver beard, and fur-lined cloak are full of nothing but cold, hard edges. You'd think he was Pop's frozen, skinny evil twin. And now that I think about it, maybe he is. They both hail from Immortal stock, after all.

"So, Jack," my father says as he gestures for me to enter, "Have you finally returned home to admit the error of your ways and take your place within the *family*?"

We've been down this ski slope before. I ignore the question. "What do you know about Santa?"

"I hear he's fat and relatively jolly."

"Don't try to snow-job me, Old Man. Santa's missing—kidnapped right out of the castle."

"Yes. I've heard. I've also heard Alfie's got Frankie the Gobbler in lock-up over it as we speak."

"Then you may have also heard I think that's nutcrackers—that the real kidnapper or kidnappers escaped without a trace—*thanks to your snowstorm.*"

The Old Man cocks a frosted, pointy eyebrow and smiles. "Am I being accused...*son?*"

"You're too smart to have loused up the crime scene. But no one does anything at the Pole without your okay."

The Old Man guffaws at this and the winds that have been blowing outside rise to hurricane strength.

"Really Jack," he says once he's regained composure, "you give me too much credit. Your father is Old Man Winter, but he's not the end-all-be-all of this realm...*or any other.*"

"What are you saying?"

"I'm saying there are powers in the holiday worlds that are not beholden to your Old Man—forces that are beyond even my censure or reproach."

I sigh. "You're not going to tell me what you know, are you?"

Old Man Winter leans out of his throne and gives me the Frosty Eye. Not to freeze me, which would pretty much be impossible, but to let me know how serious he is.

"Jack—*son*—I've told you plenty."

His gaze leaves me as he straightens in his chair. "Bominable will show you out."

Alone, without out aid, Jack set out to roam,
In the Pole's badlands, a place he once called home.
Over snowdrift and slope, he skated to find,
A dastardly suspect of an unusual kind.

Jack was almost there when he looked up to see,
A vision so scary he wanted to flee!
Bominable the monster came cracking his whip,
On his shoulder, he bore Jack a chip.

Off to Old Man Winter's castle they went,
To see this crime boss so crooked and bent.
All the way there Bominable did Jack bother,
About Old Man Winter being Frost's real father!

"That may be true," Jack said. "But he didn't raise me.
"It was Santa Claus himself who swooped in and saved me.
"He took me for his son, him and his wife,
"To love and cherish and keep free from strife."

They found Winter sitting upon his throne,
His gaze so cold it chilled even Jack's bones!
"Where is Santa?" is what Jack said.
But Winter didn't know and Jack began to feel dread.

CHAPTER 4

"Nutcrackers!" I reach the igloo and find that, not only is my new furry little friend still hanging around, but he's made himself perfectly at home. In other words, the place is trashed.

"Hey, skate out of here, you!"

The cub looks up from the snow cone he's pilfered from the icebox and tilts his head at me quizzically.

"Jingle all the way out of here, right now!"

He glances at me another second, gives a small bark, and then returns to the snow cone.

"Yeah, I need a drink, too."

I wade through the fish now carpeting my floor to get some eggnog from the icebox. Hey, why not? It's Christmas Eve somewhere—everywhere, in fact, forever and ever unless I can break this case.

I take the eggnog carton from the icebox and turn it up. It's sweet going down my throat and the dull pounding I've had in my head since the evening begins to soften.

I wipe my mouth and ponder my visit with the Old Man. I don't think he's behind this. Pop is one of the few legitimate outfits the Old Man is associated with, and he wouldn't want to ruin that. You don't sleet where you eat, after all. And Pop being gone means bad business for the Old Man.

But there's something he's not telling me. That's obvious.

The snow-globe jingles but I let the recorder catch it. Alfie's shouting voice begins to echo throughout the igloo.

"Frost! I've got feds crawling all over the castle. If I find out you're the one who called them—!"

I glide over to a window of clear ice to watch the aurora borealis through the falling snow. It always helps me think. I take another sip of eggnog.

I've told you plenty, the Old Man said. I didn't hear him say anything unless you count all that caroling about *powers beyond him.*

Was that his way of saying someone outside of the *family* was behind Pop's disappearance? Someone powerful enough not only to kidnap Santa here on my father's turf without his aid, but to force the Old Man to keep quiet about it? Chris Cringle! If that's the case, this little snow storm just got upgraded to a blizzard!

The globe jingles again and a female voice, one low and sultry, sashays out of its speakers. "Jack. It's Dee. Jack I just heard. I'm so—"

I whirl and skate over to the globe. "Dee," I say as I snatch it up. It's a voice call only—no image. Dee always was one to keep to the shadows.

"Jack," there's relief when her voice comes again. "Jack, I thought you weren't home."

"I'm here in frost if not in spirit. I guess you're calling about Pop?"

"Yes. I called to tell you how sorry I am. But the mayor also wanted me to let you know he was furious when he heard—both about the kidnapping and the fact that Alfie didn't call it in. The larger ramifications of Santa's disappearance place this under Holiday Town jurisdiction, after all."

"What can I say? You know Alfie."

"The mayor sent the *Holiday Guard* down to take over the case immediately. But he'd like to hear your thoughts."

"His honor's interested in what little ol' me has to say?"

"Please, Jack. He knows how good you are. I've made sure of it."

"And here I thought we'd agreed to never kiss and tell."

There's a long pause before Dee responds. "Those were good times, weren't they, Jack?"

"The best, Dee."

"Will you come, Jack?"

"For you, Dee. Always."

There's another long pause. "I'll tell him to expect you. Goodbye, Jack."

She hangs up before I can return the farewell. I take another pull off the eggnog and stare off into the Northern Lights. It's been over a century since I last saw Dee and I'd be lying if I said hearing her voice didn't rattle me. Family and friends are good at doing that to you. Especially over the holidays. And this is turning out to be a Christmas for the books.

I turn up the last of the eggnog and head for the icebox. "Keep the home-fires extinguished while I'm gone," I say to the polar bear cub as I go. He's engrossed in a half-frozen cod and pays me no mind.

I take a *forever carrot* out of the icebox. I've it had since the last time I went down the *Bunny Trail*. Then I exit the igloo. I notice the storm's begun to let up and decide to take it as a good omen.

I put my fingers to my mouth and give a whistle that carries for miles. *Ice and snow aren't the only talents in my bag of tricks.* A few moments pass before I hear the faint jingle of bells in the distance. Seconds later, I see something flying down through the sky. It lands in front of me and trots over on four legs.

"Hey, *Flash*, old boy!" I say as I pet the reindeer's neck and feed it the forever carrot. He finishes it in two bites and then nuzzles against my chest. It will simply be easier to get around Holiday Town with Flash. Plus, you haven't lived until you've rocketed through the aurora borealis on a flying reindeer!

I climb on Flash's back and he lets out a deep grunt.

"Hey, no fair. I've thawed five pounds since last winter!"

I take Flash's jingling reigns in my hands. "Giddiup!" I say. He doesn't move.

"Up, up, and away!" Nothing.

"Please?" Flash shakes his head, jingling his reigns. "You're going to make me say it aren't you?"

Flash nods.

"Oh, come on, Flash. I mean, this is ridiculous! I don't under-stand why we always have to..."

Flash paws the snow in impatience. I sigh in defeat and bark the words.

Now, Flasher! On, Flasher! The fastest reindeer!
To the yonder blue, without any fear!
To the top of the clouds! To the sky so high!
Now Flash away! FLash away! Flash away! Fly!"

We leave the ground so fast a trail of snow a mile long follows us in the vacuum created in Flash's wake. We go supersonic and the boom shakes the frost from both my clothes and Flash's fur.

We dive into the lights and it's like being inside a Fourth of July fireworks show. How long we're in there surfing the light streams, I don't know. Minutes? Days? Eons? It could be any of those.

But when Flash breaks out the other side, it feels like coming off the world's craziest rollercoaster. My head keeps swimming and body keeps shaking, neither convinced the ride's over. My mind finally freezes still again and I smile as I take in a flying reindeer's eye view of Holiday Town at night.

How can I begin to describe Holiday Town? Imagine an entire city made up of gigantic Bavarian castles, Asian temples, and Egyptian pyramids. Now imagine it lit up like a Christmas tree with electronic billboards, flashing neon signs, and swaying floodlight beams and you being to get the picture.

It's a wondrous thing to behold at night, like the biggest field of fireflies you've ever seen. Don't think I haven't seriously considered moving my office to this side of the aurora borealis. But things being what they are, I couldn't afford the cooling bill.

Flash is halfway through a spiraling arc around H-Town when I see two *incoming* streaking upward to meet us.

"We've got company, Flash."

The reindeer grunts.

Seconds later, two butterfly-winged fairies with Holiday Guard sashes are flying alongside us.

Feds.

Unlike their distant cousins, the Christmas elves, feds are naturally long and lean to the point of frailty. However, their looks are deceiving. They are powerhouses of magic, and *very, very dangerous.*

"Hello, Mr. Frost," the female fed, apparently the senior officer, says. "I hope you had a pleasant *tesseract* through the *nexus.* His Honor the mayor sent us to escort you to City Hall."

"Awful lot of fuss for a Pole P.I. and his reindeer." I say.

"His Honor wants to see you right away," the male chimes in, "And what his Honor wants, his Honor gets."

"Well," I say throwing up my hands in surrender, "far be it from me to deny *his Honor.* Lead the way."

Back to his igloo, Jack did skate,
To mull things over and concentrate.
His father's kidnapper he had to find,
So the wheels in his head he began to grind

Who benefits? That was the question here,
One which Jack Frost considered in fear.
There were dots to connect, gaps to bridge.
"Nutcrackers!" Jack said. "The cub's emptied my fridge!"

Just right then the snow globe rang,
With a call from Dee, giving Jack heart pangs.
He scooped up the phone to answer his old flame.
She was a mysterious girl, a real classy dame.

"Oh, Jack," Dee said, "City Hall wants to help you,
"Find Santa Claus and stop this coup."
"I'm on my way," Jack said, "to Holiday Town,
"As soon as the Flash the flying reindeer can be found."

Jack whistled for his four-legged ride,
To fly through him the borealis as his guide.
Up and away they went through the vortex,
In H-Town was where they landed next.

CHAPTER 5

Flash and I plummet until we're only a few stories above the streets. We level off and twist and turn at high velocity between buildings, turrets, streamers, and decorations until we reach City Hall. We land at the steps and I dismount Flash.

"Stay close, boy," I say as I pat his neck. "I'll be back in a little while."

He grunts and then is off like a shot to find some grass to munch.

"This way, please," the senior fed gestures toward the entrance.

Another female fed with teal blue wings and a scanning wand awaits us just inside the door. I enter and she passes the wand up one side of me and then down the other, scanning me for black magic. Satisfied I'm carrying none, she hands me a visitor's badge and ushers me farther into the building.

My fairy escorts take positions on either side of me and lead me through a large, cathedral-like foyer to one of two elevators on the room's other side. We pass by numerous paintings and busts of Holiday Town mayors past on our way there. The going is slower than usual for me since I don't have ice and snow to skate over.

We reach the elevator and I notice that, instead of numbers, the buttons to the various floors are labeled with epochs that range from *big bang* to *present day*. As you can imagine, there are quite a lot more buttons available here than on your typical elevator—far more than the building's outward appearance would indicate. Fairy magic at work.

"Cool!" I say as I start to reach for a button labeled *Renaissance*.

The senior fed slaps my hand away. "You are not authorized to use the time-evator!"

I shrug as the junior fed hits the button for present day. We bullet upward, the different floors passing us like stripes on a human highway. Moments later, the time-evator reaches our floor and slams to a halt. You'd expect the momentum would've of made us all greasy spots on the ceiling. But, once again, thanks to fairy magic, that's not the case.

The time-evator doors open to reveal a gigantic room, every time piece imaginable adorning its walls. But that's not what takes my breath away. It's the sight of Dee.

She's as beautiful as ever, even dressed in her executive power-suit—*black of course*. The matching hat and half-veil make her look more suited for a funeral than a day in the office, though. But then, what else would you expect from a *Halloweenian*?

The initial shock of seeing her fades, and I realize she's seated upon the mayor's desk. She's facing away from him, but leaning back to whisper something in his ear. It's the kind of closeness I once shared with her and I am instantly jealous of *his Honor.*

"Hello, Delilah," I say and they finally notice the feds and I are in the room.

"Jack," Dee walks toward me with wide, welcoming arms.

I stick my hand out for her to shake. She bypasses it and squeezes her arms around me.

"Oh, Jack! I'm so glad you came."

She smells of candied apples and autumn breezes. Old Habits take over and my arms cover her like snow blanketing the ground. She pulls away from me and I feel like a human who's had his winter-coat snatched off him while in the middle of a blizzard.

The mayor clears his throat from his new position behind Dee.

"Oh, where are my manners?" Dee says. "Jack, this is the mayor, *Father Time.*"

Father Time looks just like you'd expect—ancient. Long, flowing robes—*check*. Long, white beard—*check*. A crown of holly—*check*. Magical staff with the hourglass head—*double check*.

"Pleased to meet you, Mr. Frost," Father Time says as he shakes my hand.

"Likewise," I say, and before I can help myself, "How is your lovely *wife*, these days?"

If he perceives my verbal jab, he shows no sign of it. In fact, his face turns quite forlorn.

"Oh, Mother Nature is taking this whole mess quite badly, I'm afraid, what with the birth of Baby New Year now being indefinitely on hold."

"The spell of eternal night, Jack," Dee clarifies. "The New Year can't very well ring in until Christmas passes, after all."

What an insensitive snowflake I am! I mentally kick myself. His family is suffering from this, just like mine. And Dee is Father Time's assistant. It is only natural they would be close.

"I'm so sorry to hear that," I say.

"It's quite alright, Jack. May I call you Jack?"

"Certainly, your honor."

"Please! Call me *FT*."

Father Time's sadness turns to concern and he places a hand on my shoulder. "But I'm being selfish. I can only imagine how hard it is for your own father to have been kidnapped."

"It's been hardest for Mom." I say.

"Yes, of course," Time says. "Jack, the state of our families— and the state of time in general—is precisely why I wanted to see you."

He gestures toward Dee. "Delilah has told me about all the cases you've solved at the North Pole."

"They weren't so hard to solve, your honor. Nine times out of ten it was the Awgwas to blame."

"And humble, too!" Father Time says beaming at Dee, "Oh, I like this boy, Dee."

Smiling like that, Father Time reminds me somewhat of Pop, and I think how it's hard not to warm to this man—in the non-literal sense, of course.

"He's not so bad once you get to know him," Dee says smiling at me. My heart lights up like a Christmas tree.

"Anyway, your prowess as an investigator is why I'd like you to partner with City Hall on this case."

THE LONG SILENT NIGHT

Whoa. That came out of left-field. "What, me? I don't know. Anyway, can't you just hop in that time-evator back there and see who did kidnap my pop?"

"Normally, yes." Father Time says, "But I'm afraid, the time-evator's magic is having some glitches where the past few days are concerned. We should be able to work out the bugs in a century or two.

"But anyway, who better to solve a kidnapping at the North Pole than its premiere detective!"

"I appreciate the offer your honor—"

"FT."

"Uh, FT, really I do. But you see, I don't do well taking orders. And red tape tends to make me want to melt."

Dee shrugs her shoulders. "I told you he was bull-headed."

Father Time looks at me and sighs. "You're certain you won't reconsider? Technically, you'd still be a civilian and so still eligible for the sizeable reward City Hall is offering—?"

"The offer's tempting, FT, really. But I do my best work alone."

"Very well," Father Time says at last. He gestures toward fairy fed senior. She's stood like a statue by the door with her partner all this time. "At least stay long enough to discuss any leads you may have with my senior officers,"

Dee looks at her watch. "It will have to be after the press conference. Jasmine and Romeo are on security detail."

The feds, now named as Jasmine and Romeo, nod in unison.

"Of course," Father Time says. He keeps talking, but I lose the rest of his words as I glance at Dee from the corner of my eye. She is in a silent, dreamlike world before me, her head nodding and her lips moving in slow motion.

Somewhere deep in the back of my mind, a small voice tells me I should stop staring. If I'm ever going to find Pop, I've got to keep my head free of distractions. But that voice is quickly silenced by the unyielding song the vision of Dee creates inside me.

Up to the mayor's office Jack rode,
To speak with Father Time in his abode.
He made the trip in a time-evator.
It can time-travel back, forward, to now or later.

Dee was there, whispering in Father Time's ear.
It made Jack want to kick the mayor's rear!
But then Jack wanted to kick himself,
For being an insensitive frosty elf.

Jack was hurt with his Pop gone,
But his wasn't the only sad song.
Father Time also had reason to mourn
His son, Baby New Year, couldn't be born.

For unless Santa ended the spell of eternal night,
The Christmas dawn would never light.
Time would stand still forever and ever,
With no shifting of seasons or changing of weather.

"So listen, Jack, here's the situation:
"We want you to lead City Hall's investigation."
"Thanks for the offer," Jack said, "I know it's heartfelt.
"But government red-tape simply makes me melt!"

CHAPTER 6

The press room is a large auditorium—one already brimming with reporters from all the Holiday worlds and several others. I take a spot against a wall near the front. The cameras of bunny rabbits, cupids, and vamps flash like unending machine gun fire as Father Time joins Dee, Jasmine, Romeo, and a very sad and pregnant Mother Nature on stage. He takes his place behind a podium and speaks into the horn of plenty mounted atop it.

"Ladies and gentlemen of the press, members of City Council, and friends viewing at home, thank you all for giving of your precious time to hear me today.

"As many of you may already know, we, the members of the known worlds, currently face one of the most desperate crises to have occurred on record. *Santa Claus has been kidnapped.*"

Murmurs run throughout the room like an electric current. Father Time raises a single hand and, after several moments, the room quiets once more.

"Our hearts go out to Santa, his family, his reindeer, and his elves. If that were all that faced us this day, that would truly be severe enough. However, I'm saddened to say that is not the extent of our problems.

"When Santa was taken, he had already invoked the spell of eternal night—a spell given to him by my forefathers generations ago—in order to go about his good works on Christmas Eve.

"I'm afraid, until Santa can be found, and the last present delivered to the last human boy and girl, time will be effectively frozen and the shadow of night will cover us indefinitely."

Fear and confusion in the form of alarmed chatter spread through the room once more. I suddenly feel a slight draft of cold air, one imperceptible to everyone else. But *cold* is my life's blood and I feel its presence in any form, no matter how minute. I sense its origin in the balcony and scan the area.

"In kidnapping Santa," Father Time continues, "these terrorists—I call them terrorists, for in perpetrating this attack upon Santa they have perpetrated an attack upon my family, the peoples of the known worlds, and time itself—must be brought to justice at any cost!"

The balcony windows are all closed. The draft couldn't have come from there. There must be something else. Something I'm overlooking.

"I'm glad to report," Father Time continues, "our police forces in the North Pole have already apprehended a suspect for questioning.

"I regret such a tragedy has occurred in this late hour of my tenure as the people's servant—a time when I should've been able to take some much needed rest. However, rest assured, I pledge to do what must be done and stay in office as long as it takes to bring the guilty parties to justice!"

The press rises to its feet and applause erupts around the room. It's at this moment I see the open grate of an air conditioning duct dangling from the ceiling. A black-and-white clad pilgrim stands directly below it, aiming a horn-ended musket at Father Time.

"Death to Christmas!" the pilgrim shouts. "Death to the oppressors!"

"Gun!" I scream just as the Pilgrim fires his weapon.

To her credit, Jasmine moves like a bolt of lightning, tackling Father Time to the ground in just enough time for the musket ball to miss its intended target and clip her wing. The room descends into chaos. Holiday archetypes begin running and screaming, trampling over one another in effort to flee.

Romeo rockets up into the balcony only to receive a whack across the head with the musket stock for his trouble. It knocks him cold. The pilgrim drops the weapon and crashes through one of the balcony windows to escape. I give Dee a quick glance.

She is helping the mayor sit up while Mother Nature tends to Jasmine's wound.

"Go!" Dee shouts.

I don't have to be told twice.

In the blink of an eye, I form an ice ramp leading to the balcony and skate up it for the window. The act taxes the majority of my magic. It's a risky move without the Pole's arctic climate outside to replenish me, but it's the only way to close the distance to the pilgrim before he can get away.

In the moonlight, I see the pilgrim racing across rooftops in the distance at speeds normally impossible for a human archetype. I give chase.

Being of fairy, after a fashion, I'm able to achieve greater than normal feats of speed and strength myself. In no time, I've closed the gap to only a few yards between us. But his leaping ability is still superior to mine, and he knows it. He chooses a path that takes us over a series of towers, the distance between them spreading farther apart with each one.

I struggle to make each leap, but he jumps along as though it were a piece of fruitcake. At last, I'm able to seize the back of his white, puritan collar. But I realize my hold has come at a price, for I look down to see that, in aiming for the pilgrim, I've sacrificed my footing.

The white collar rips off of the pilgrim's neck and I begin to flail in the air as the ground rushes up to meet me. The fingers of my left hand unexpectedly find a hold on the tower-top edge and my body cracks like a whip. I look down to see I'm dangling by one hand hundreds of stories above the earth.

I catch the putrid scent of wet dog on the air and look up to see the pilgrim, his face masked by shadow, staring down at me.

"Give up and I'll go easy on you." I say.

I realize he's unimpressed with my sarcasm when he places his black leather boot down on my hand, forcing me to release my hold. I yell in pain and drop.

"Sorry, Pop," I whisper. Then I whistle like my life depends on it, knowing full well that it does. I hear the faint jingle of bells in the distance and smile.

Down to the press room, they traveled in twos,
To fill in reporters on the bad news.
"Santa Claus has been kidnapped," Father Time said,
"Stolen from his home, ripped out of his bed!"

At his words, the crowd did roar.
"What else do you know? Tell us more!"
"I'm afraid it's worse," Father Time said forthright.
"Time has been frozen in the long silent night!"

Is was right then that Jack noticed,
A breeze in the room that was the coldest.
He saw its source, thanks to his luck.
An assassin had sneaked in through an AC duct.

"Gun!" Jack shouted, but it was too late.
The assassin fired, sealing the mayor's fate.
But at the last second, a fairy saved the day,
The gun shot missed. Hip-hip-hooray!

Jack chased the assassin across the rooftop,
But the evil pilgrim would not stop.
Jack grabbed his collar, ripping it off,
But it made him fall from high aloft!

CHAPTER 7

"I don't know what I'd have done without you, boy," I say as I stroke the back of Flash's head. "It's all the reindeer moss you want when we get back to the pole!"

"Jack!" Dee calls as she rushes out onto the City Hall steps to speak with me, "We saw you fall! I was so scared!"

She flings herself into my arms and I feel like a kid on Christmas morning.

"If it hadn't been for Flash's Superman act back there," I say, "this ice cube would've been crushed into a slushy!" We release each other. "We circled back up to look for the pilgrim—gone like a groundhog who's seen his shadow."

"We've got the Holiday Guard scouring the city," Dee confides. "Another squad has been dispatched to the Thanksgiving world. The mayor may declare martial law over there before this is all over. Who knew their hatred for Christmas ran so deep?"

"Any prints on the gun or at the scene?"

Dee shakes her head.

"Figures."

I look down at the collar I snatched from the pilgrim. I managed to keep hold of it even during my fall. There's an unusual amount of fine, dark hairs lining its surface.

"Jack, is something wrong?"

"It's—" I say, considering my words, "probably nothing, Dee. Just a hunch."

"What kind of hunch?" Dee asks.

I ignore the question.

"Look, I need to get back to the Pole. Call me if anything turns up. Okay?"

Dee nods and plants a kiss on my cheek. If I could, I'd be blushing right now.

"Jack—"

"Yeah, Dee?"

"Be careful."

I give Dee one long, last look as she turns and walks away. Then I mount Flash and before you can say 'Merry Christmas,' we're flying out the Pole side of the aurora borealis.

The cold hits my face and I immediately feel like myself again, full of sleet and snow. I ask Flash to hang around while I make a pit stop by my igloo to make sure the polar bear cub hasn't totally eaten me out of house and home.

Of course, he has.

The cub sits in the middle of my living room, pawing at his stuffed belly.

"Can I get you anything else?" I ask. "A Christmas goose? Perhaps a full grown buffalo would be more to your liking?"

My sarcasm is lost on him.

I pick up the snow globe and call Mom.

"Hello?"

"Mom. It's Jack."

"Jack! I saw Father Time's press conference on the globe! Are you okay?"

"I'm fine, Mom."

"Thank Great Ak! I was so worried! Did they catch the shooter?"

"I'm afraid not, Mom. He got away. But I've got a lead, so don't you worry. It's going to be okay. *I promise.*"

"I—" Mom says, not sounding too convinced, "I know you're doing your best, son. I'll always love you and be proud of you, no matter what happens."

"I'm going to find him, Mom."

"Jack?"

"Yeah, Mom?"

"Your father would be proud of you, too. He always was."

"I know."

"I love you Jack."

"I know."

I end the call and stare down at the pilgrim's collar in my hand, once again noticing the hairs lining its surface. Proper procedure would've been to turn it over to the feds to check out. But I didn't want to risk them fouling it up. Not when Pop's life may be at stake.

I make another call on the globe.

"Speak!" A faceless voice commands from the other end.

"Fred, it's Jack."

"Yo, what up, J?"

"I need your help."

"Well, homie, I got the skills to pay the bills! Know what I'm sayin'?"

"I'll be there in fifteen...*Ugh! What's that smell?*"

I look up to see my apparently new roommate standing near the wall with one furry leg hiked up as he marks his territory. He turns and looks at me and I swear he's grinning.

"Nutcrackers!"

Jack brought up his hands and whistled for his life,
And Flash the reindeer sliced through the air like a knife!
He rocketed through the sky to heed Jack's call.
Flash saved the elf, stopping his fall!

"Jack! You made it!" Dee said, "I'm glad you're okay.
"Flash the flying reindeer really saved the day!"
"That he did," Jack said, "But the perp got away.
"I've got to track him down without delay!"

So Jack rode home, the pilgrim's collar in his hand,
"If this clue breaks the case, it sure would be grand!"
Back inside his igloo, Jack made a few calls.
The cub had trashed his house; floor, ceiling, and walls.

"Yo! What's up?" said the voice on the globe's other end.
"Funk Master Fred, I've got some work for you, my friend."
Jack turned to leave but what he saw had him booing
The little bear cub in his living room was pooing!

Jack broke out the towels, disinfectants, and sprays,
Without out a doubt, his home had seen better days.
"You better be glad you're still just a pup,
"Or I'd have you scrubbing this mess and cleaning it up!"

CHAPTER 8

Fred, or *Funk Master Fred*, as he currently prefers to be called, is not your normal Christmas elf. He is a true prodigy, and by happenstance, a virtual outcast among his own kind.

Computers? Video Games? Humans may have created them, but it was Fred who perfected them (*Heck, he created the cure for iron sickness all magical beings suffer from. That's why the elves are able to build mechanical toys. Next time Santa puts a Transformer under your tree, thank Fred!*).

You see, Fred has always been fascinated with humans. They have been his muse and teacher now for millennia. He even tries to pattern himself after them. He spent their dark ages running around in kingly robes, *doth-ing* this and *thou-ing* that. During their 1960's, he wore a modest suit and tie and told everyone *not to ask what their Christmas could do for them, but what they could do for their Christmas!"*

In recent decades, he's discovered what the humans call *hip-hop*. I'm not sure what that means. You'd think it involved jumping, but I've yet to see Fred take the first leap. Instead, he tends to wear baggy clothes and gaudy jewelry and say "Yo" a lot. But eccentricity is just part of the genius package, I suppose.

I reach Fred's house in the village surrounding Christmas Castle and knock.

"Who knocks, yo?" Fred's voice calls from the other side of the door.

"It's Frost. Open up."

The door opens in front of me, releasing light into the nighttime darkness. "Yo, J-Dog!" Fred is not dressed in typical toymaker attire. No, he's Funk-mastered-out in sheeny red warm-up gear and what he refers to as *bling*. And his green cap is on backwards, of course.

Upon greeting, he insists in doing what he calls *bumping fists* and hugs me in a very awkward way. I return both gestures as I'm used to this odd behavior by now.

"Step on up to my crib, J."

I enter Fred's house and hear the thumping bass and indiscernible chanting that's always playing in the background when I visit.

"You like that, J?" Fred says, noticing me noticing the noise. "It's the new Crunk X joint."

"Crunk X?"

"He's a rapper."

"Then why's he making that awful noise? We can always use gift wrappers here at the Pole, after all."

"Yo," Fred says, laughing, "You're whacked, J!"

"Whacked? No one's hit me. However, I did take a nasty fall, earlier."

Fred rolls his eyes dismissingly and sits down at his computer. "Yo, I was just kicking it RPG-style before you came in."

"I'm afraid to ask."

"Never mind, J. It ain't no thing. What's up?"

I hold out the pilgrim's collar for Fred to take. He does and sniffs it.

"Yo, this smells like wet dog."

I shrug. "A pilgrim wearing this tried to ice Father Time."

"For real?"

"For real."

"Yo! That's some hardcore gangster—" Fred glances up at me sheepishly, catching himself. My heritage haunts me as ever.

"I think it has to do with Pop's kidnapping. Or, at least, that's what I'm supposed to think."

"Yeah, I heard about that. Yo, that's whacked! Whatever I can do to help, know what I'm saying?"

"See those hairs on the collar?"

"Word."

"I thought you could check them out under that fancy eye of yours."

"The microscope? You got it, J."

I follow Fred out of the front room into his workshop—a place that would make any human Einstein or Gates-types jealous. We reach the microscope and, after a bit of tinkering, Fred places a slide of the hairs from the collar beneath its lens. He adjusts the microscope's knobs as he peers down through it at the magnified follicles. I watch as Fred's jaw drops.

"Yo, check it!"

"Whatcha got?"

Fred looks up from the microscope and gestures for me to give him a second. He searches through a few of the drawers in his bench until he pulls out a long, dark, halogen bulb. He presses a button along its housing and the bulb glows an eerie blue-black.

"This bulb is designed to give out ultraviolet light, like the sun." Fred slips out of hip-hop mode without realizing it. It always happens when he gets technical. That's when the real Fred shines through.

"Sunlight. Got it."

"Now watch." Fred holds the bulb over the Pilgrim's collar where it lies on the bench. It's once white surface now glows the same blue-black as the light.

"I don't follow you."

"Look closer...   ."

I lean in and peer at the hairs lining the collar. I feel my brow furrow as I watch them literally shrink under the ultraviolet light.

"Yo, this collar didn't come from no pilgrim, J."

"Yeah?"

"The wet dog smell; the hairs shrinking under the UV-light—I hate to tell you this, but it looks like you got a Halloweenian on your hands, J—a lycanthrope."

"Lycanthrope?"

"A werewolf."

"I was afraid you'd say that. *Very afraid.*"

Still at the Pole, Jack went to Fred's pad,
For he needed some help finding his Dad.
Now Funkmaster Fred wasn't your typical elf.
After the humans of the world, he patterned himself.

He'd been a doctor, a lawyer, a fireman too.
Now he was a rapper of the hip-hop crew.
In all things scientific was where Fred's true talents lay.
He was the elf who invented the mechanized sleigh.

Jack had come to borrow Fred's smarts,
To find his father using scientific arts.
"Can you help me out?" Jack asked with hope.
"You know it," Fred said, "My skills are dope!"

"Look at this collar," Jack said, "If you don't mind.
"Give it a once over. See what you can find."
Into his microscope, Funkmaster Fred gazed.
What he saw left him quite phased.

"Yo, J, check it! Do you see these hairs?
"They don't belong to a human, but a creature who scares!
"That wasn't any pilgrim who shot at the mayor.
"It was a werewolf, dog! A Halloweenian, player!"

CHAPTER 9

Nutcrackers! This is bad. *Very bad*. But then, it always is when you get Halloweenians involved. They make the long departed Awgwas look like kindergarteners by comparison.

The October Country government is token—so corrupt one wonders why they even bother. It's *Samhain* and his crew in Necropolis who really run things. And if Santa's kidnapping and the botched hit on Father Time reaches to his level, well, this is going to get even uglier!

Not that all Halloweenians are bad people, though. In fact, in my rebellious youth, I spent some time in the October Country— more to spite the Old Man than anything. Unfortunately, it broke Mom and Pop's hearts, too. But I eventually got out. Most of the good ones do. Take Dee, for instance. She couldn't put the October Country in her rearview mirror fast enough, *to use a human expression*. She was always meant for bigger and better things and she knew it.

I bid Fred goodbye and ride Flash through the Northern Lights for Holiday Town once more. H-Town was built in the nexus between all worlds and serves specifically as the gateway between the different holiday realms.

I make a mental note that when all this is chilled and frozen, I'm going to have to rethink moving my office over here to cut down on the commute, if nothing else.

Plus, the fact that I'd be closer to Dee wouldn't hurt.

We fly through the night around City Hall until I spot Dee talking on a crystal ball through her office window. We pull alongside and I knock. She jerks her head around, startled, then relaxes when she sees it's me.

I see her mouth the words, *I'll have to call you back,* and then the crystal ball goes dim. She gets up from her desk and opens the window.

"Bad time?" I ask.

"Right this minute or in general?"

"Yeah, right."

"Well, don't just hang out there like an icicle. Come on in."

"Love to. But I've got places to be. That hunch I was telling you about…"

"Yeah?"

"Came up silver and gold. The pilgrim get-up was all for show, like the feathers in Pop's bedroom. Dee, the shooter was from your world. We're dealing with a Halloweenian."

"Oh my! What are you going to do?"

"Go to the October Country. Sniff around. See what snow I can shovel up."

"Oh, Jack, do be careful. If you stir the wrong cauldron there—!"

"Don't worry. Remember, I've been Halloween side before."

The pale flesh of her cheeks fills with color. "Of course I remember. How could I ever forget?"

I place my hand beneath her chin, holding it between thumb and forefinger. She tilts her head to the side, cradling my hand against her shoulder. We release one another and, without another word between us, Flash carries me away for the H-Town cemetery.

Flash halts at the gate of spiked black iron, refusing to go any farther. "I don't blame you, boy." I pet his neck. "Go find you some food. Check back every so often. If I'm not back after you've had three meals, go home." Flash huffs and then is off like a shooting star.

I turn and survey the cemetery. On the other side of the fence, gnarled trees and broken tombstones rise from a lake of eerie mist. I'm definitely on the edge of October Country.

I open the gate and wade into the mist. I reach the crumbling, marble tomb serving as the cemetery's heart and shove my way past the Tomb's stone slab of a door. The tomb's ceiling has long fallen in, so in the moonlight it's easy to see all the creepy-crawlers skittering about the piles of bones they've claimed for house and home. I make my way to an ancient stone sarcophagus rising out of the earth at the tomb's center. It serves as the door to the October Country. With considerable effort I push open its lid and look inside. A gaping mouth of darkness lies before me as deep as the eye can see. It gives even me chills.

I climb inside, my feet landing on descending stairs. I move forward and the stairs soon peter out for earthen floor. This is the opposite of traveling through the Northern Lights. I sense things moving far out in the darkness around me—enormous, nameless things older than time itself. I try not to think what would happen if I lost my way and came face to face with one of them.

I breathe a sigh of relief when I see a pinprick of dim light ahead in the distance. Soon, the light has enlarged to the point I can see it's the mouth of a cave—one I'm now in. When I exit, the first thing I notice is the gigantic moon hanging bright and full in the night sky. It shines down upon *Necropolis*—a city of haunted Victorian mansions and tall, gothic cathedrals huddled away from the forest in the valley below.

The howl of a wolf goes up into the night. It turns my attention to Samhain's base of operations—a twisting black castle that crests the opposite side of the valley. Great Ak help me if I have to cross his path!

"For Pop," I tell myself and then start down the mountainside for the village.

Jack gathered his courage and swallowed his pride,
For he had to journey Halloween-side.
"This just got worse," Jack said as he went,
"The Halloween monsters have wicked intent."

But that's not exactly true, Jack then thought.
Dee's done very well, for a better life she's fought.
Speaking of the Devil, Jack wanted to see her.
So he went to City Hall and was pleased to meet her.

"What's the latest, Jack? Tell me what you have learned."
"The pilgrim was a wolf, Dee. My attention, he has earned."
"So what will you do?" Dee asked. "It's not clear to me."
"Go to Necropolis," Jack said, "And see what I can see."

To the H-Town cemetery Jack then traveled,
Into a tomb of crumbling block and gravel.
Down into its stone sarcophagus he went,
Deep in the darkness where time and space are rent.

When Jack emerged, he shivered in fear,
For the haunted town of Necropolis was now very near.
Keep it together, Jack thought. Don't let your nerve drop!
Then Jack strode into Necropolis, looking for his Pop.

CHAPTER 10

Despite it being late at night—or in this case, I suspect because of it—the cobblestone streets of Necropolis are bustling with activity. Jack-o-lanterns sit at every doorstep, each a flickering homage to the town benefactor, Samhain himself. Crowds of monsters dance and shriek while their blind-folded ghoul children beat piñatas and bob for apples.

I grab the arm of a zombie shambling by me. "What's all the jingling about?"

The zombie looks at me with sunken, glazed eyes and moans a response. "Niiiieeeght. Fooooreeeehveeeeer."

Night forever. Like I said, the Thanksgiving folk aren't the only Holidayers who would benefit from Santa's sleigh being grounded. Want suspects? How about a gazillion undead!

I hold up the pilgrim collar for the zombie to smell. "Do you know this wolf?"

He grunts in negative.

Hey, it was worth a shot.

"Thanks."

I walk away, leaving the zombie bent over, his mouth wide open where he was slowly leaning down to take a bite out of my arm.

I scan the crowd, looking for a certain acquaintance of mine from the old days. At last, I spot his hunched back at a stand offering hearts, spleens and other internal organs as snack food. I push my way through droves of ghosts, goblins, and witches and sneak up behind him, wishing to catch him off guard. I grab his arm, his filthy, ragged sleeve greasy to the touch, and spin him around.

He sees me and his one good eye goes large with shock as he drops the jar containing the brain he was holding. It shatters at our feet.

"Master!"

"Hello, Smeagor."

Without another word, I drag him out of the crowd and into an alley where we can talk in private.

"It's been so long, master!" Smeagor snivels.

"I was your boss, Smeagor. Never your master. You know that."

I'm sad to say, before I got into the P.I biz, I had a gig as a day courier for Samhain here in October Country. I only took legit work. *Honest.*

Centuries later, I realize I did it to rebel against the Old Man more than anything—*working for the competition and what not.*

Smeagor used to be one of my package carriers. He also tried to erase me from existence, but that's another story.

"Yes, master. As you say, master." Smeagor scratches the hump on his back. It's one of his many annoying nervous ticks.

I raise the collar for Smeagor to see. "I'm looking for the lycanthrope who wore this."

"Smeagor know nothing, master!"

"Don't hold out on me, Smeagor. I've known you almost a millennium, and anytime something more rotten than usual went down Halloween side, you were always smack in the middle of it!"

"Smeagor promise! Smeagor know no werewolf! Smeagor know nothing!"

"Don't make me give you the Eye, Smeagor!"

Smeagor collapses into a mass of flailing appendages trying to hide his face. "Pleassse, not the Eye, master! Not the Eye!"

"I'll do it, Smeagor! I'll do it if you don't tell me who's this is!"

No I wouldn't. He's slippery, but he's pitiful, too. I couldn't bring myself to use the Eye against him. *But what he doesn't know…*

"Yes, master!" Smeagor pleads. "Smeagor know! Smeagor take you! Please, no Eye!"

"Okay, Smeagor. No Eye."

Smeagor peeks up at him from between his folded arms. "No Eye?"

"No Eye."

Smeagor jumps to his feet, clasping my hand appreciatively in both of his as he smiles up at me.

"No Eye," he says, his breath rancid in my face. "No Eye. Smeagor take you to werewolf. No Eye."

I jerk my hand away from his. If Smeagor notices my revulsion, he doesn't show it.

He grins from ear to ear and motions for me to follow him deeper into the alleyways. "Come. Smeagor take you to werewolf."

Smeagor leads me through a network of decrepit, twisting alleys until we reach a staircase leading down into the Necropolis subway tunnels.

"Down there, master!" Smeagor says as he points at the subway entrance. "Wolf down there!"

Unlike the rail cars in the human world, these tunnels house iron beasts powered by steam and black magic—*not that I can see them in the darkness below right now.*

"You first," I command.

Smeagor hesitates a moment, then smiles and nods. This carols like a set up. But what choice do I have? Smeagor is the only solid lead I've got on the wolf-pilgrim.

He shambles down the broken steam-powered escalator and I follow. I reach into my pocket and pull out a bit of the aurora borealis I've saved from previous trips to light our way.

If I'd done that in the darkness when crossing over to Halloween side, it would've been like shouting "Dinner is served!" to the nameless things that lurk in the void. Not that it's exactly safe to do it here, but like I said, I don't have a lot of options in any case.

We reach the escalator bottom and advance into the subway proper. The ground is damp beneath our feet. These old tunnels often flood with a hard rain. It must have come a gulley-washer not long ago as I can still hear water dripping all around us.

At last, Smeagor halts.

"So where's the wolf, Smeagor?" I ask.

A growling voice in the dark answers.

"Right here!"

The electric lights snap on and I see we are surrounded in every direction by snarling werewolves. They crouch low, their fur bristling, their ears flattened against the backs of their heads, their muzzles drawn away from their fangs. The particular werewolf I'm looking for stands before a sparking breaker panel. He's still clothed in his pilgrim costume despite being fully wolfed-out.

Before I can do anything about it, Smeagor scampers over to him and crouches by his leg. The wolf-pilgrim reaches down and pets his head.

"Good boy," he snarls, never taking his eyes off me.

"Thank you, master!" Smeagor replies.

"Where is Santa Claus?" I ask the wolf-pilgrim.

He throws his head back and voices something half howl, half laughter. "You'll never see that jolly fat man again, Frost. Just be glad we have orders that this be quick and relatively painless."

He smiles, his yellow canines glistening under the lights. "Of course, I was never one to follow orders!"

The other werewolves begin to bark and creep toward me. It's now or never! I consider going dim, but realize it wouldn't do any good against those keen werewolf noses. Instead, I use my magic, freezing the damp floor so that its surface becomes a solid sheet of ice. Just in time too, for the three wolves closest to me go slipping and sliding in their botched attempts to pounce on me.

I skate quick as a flying reindeer for the stairs, dodging one spinning-out-of-control werewolf after another. I reach the stairs and scamper to the top. I spare a backward glance to see if any have made it off the ice to follow me. It's a big mistake for, just as I'm craning my neck, I feel something crash against the back of my head and then everything goes dark.

Down in Necropolis, a party was in full swing,
Due to the eternal night and the freedom it did bring.
Now all the Halloween monsters could travel around,
With no fear of sunlight keeping them bound!

"Have you seen a werewolf?" A zombie, Jack asked.
The ghoul just shrugged his shoulders and shambled past.
Then Jack saw a monster he did anything but adore.
It was his old enemy, the hunchback named Smeagor.

"Hello, master!" Smeagor said, "It's so good to see you!"
"Stop lying," Jack said, "Or this night you will rue!
"I'm looking for the wolf who wore this collar.
"If you don't help me, I'll make you holler!"

"No need to get angry" Smeagor then cried.
"I'll take you to the wolf. Let me be your guide."
Through twisting back alleys, Smeagor led Jack.
"If I take my eye off him, he'll stab me in the back!"

Suddenly, out of the shadows, a werewolf pack sprang!
"You set me up, Smeagor! I should've known! Dang!"
Jack froze the ground so the wolves couldn't creep.
But then a blow to his head put him to sleep!

CHAPTER 11

I wake up with my head pounding for the second time tonight. "Nutcrackers!" I say as I massage my scalp. "Just when I'd gotten over my last headache!"

"May we get you anything?" a voice says to me, pronouncing the word *we* like *vee*.

I'd know that exaggerated Hungarian accent anywhere. The room stops spinning before my eyes and I see by the light of several well-positioned oil lamps that I'm lying in a Victorian parlor with the Count seated beside me in a plush, high-backed chair. He's dressed to the nines, his widow's peak an oily dagger slicing its way down the middle of his pale forehead.

Lenny Frankensteinbeck stands at his side, ever the obedient guard dog.

"Hello, Count."

"Hello, Jack," the vampire replies. "Good to see you again." The Count is one of Samhain's chief lieutenants. I thank my lucky Christmas star it is only him before me and not his sister, Lilith. That's one witch you don't want to cross paths with!

I look up at the patchwork corpse and nod.

"Lenny."

"Hi, Jack!" he says, waving one huge arm at me enthusiastically. "Sorry I had to bonk you."

Despite serving as the Count's muscle, Lenny Frankensteinbeck is one of the nicest patchwork corpses you'll ever meet. In contrast to his towering, monstrous frame, Lenny has the mind of a child. It makes it easy for a master of manipulation like the Count to control him.

I turn my attention back to the Count. "You could have just said, 'Hello.' "

He shrugs. "Old habits *die* hard."

"Yeah," I say, massaging my head as I rise to sit. "I guess this is the part where I ask what horrible fate you have planned for me."

I try to sound tough, but I'm praying this isn't the last stop on my way to see Samhain.

"Please, Jack!" the Count says, feigning surprise. "Harming you is the farthest thing from our minds. In fact, it was the master himself who asked us to rescue you from that pack of werewolves."

"No doubt after he'd sicced them on me in the first place."

"No, Jack!" Lenny says shaking his head emphatically. We didn't do that! Honest!"

"Hush, Lenny!" the Count commands. Lenny hangs his enormous, block-shaped head in silence, sheepish and defeated.

"Now Jack," the Count says. "Such harsh accusations. That pack was operating outside of Samhain's authority. They will be dealt with accordingly."

"I'd like to see the pack's leader, first. He and I have *business.*"

"Alas, he alone has slipped between our claws for the moment."

"How convenient."

"*Now Jack.* I know what you are thinking. But believe me when I say it is in all our best interests that you find him. We want Santa delivering presents and the spell of eternal night lifted just as badly as you."

"Your townspeople don't seem to mind eternal night so much. They're throwing a party in celebration of it as I recall."

"Yes, but their festive attitude will be short-lived, I assure you."

"How so?"

"How much trick-or-treating do you think can be done with the human children asleep in their beds for all eternity? It's bad for business. And bad business is something the master absolutely will not tolerate."

"I see your point. So where does that leave us?"

"We want to help you, Jack." the Count reaches a bony, tal-oned hand into his coat and produces a photograph. He hands it to me. In it, a dark, handsome man with bushy eyebrows is hugging a beautiful woman in white robes.

"The wolf in question's name is Larry Talbot," the Count says. "That's him in his human form. The lady he's hugging is his on again, off again girlfriend, Lupercalia Lovelace. She's a Valentiner."

"And?"

"Larry has to know October Country isn't safe for him any-more. We've searched every cave and grave Halloween side, but haven't found a trace of him. He's had to have gone on the lam, and chances are it's Valentine side with her."

"So go there and get him."

The Count raises his eyebrows in shock and revulsion. "With all that horrid love and affection everywhere? You must be joking!

"*Fear*, not love, is our unlife's blood. Hardcore Halloweenians in the Valentine world? It would be like asking you to search for Talbot in the tropics!

"Yeah, yeah. But I suppose it *is* me you're asking to go take a look, huh?"

"Was that not what you were doing already? Samhain would be most appreciative. It broke the master's heart when you left us. He could really use your help. Now and *later.*"

"Oh yeah?"

"Both your skills as a P.I. and your abilities as an elemen-tal would be very beneficial to the master. Especially should he ever wish to *expand* his operations."

"Do tell?" I say. I stand up, already knowing where this is going.

The Count also rises to his feet.

"Your Old Man can't stay a boss forever. I'm sure it's because he sees his eventual replacement in you that he treats you with such disrespect.

"What if I were to say we could help hasten your ascension to your Old Man's throne?"

I fold my arms as my gaze frosts over. "You put October

Country's muscle behind me to overthrow Winter and all I have to do in return is be Samhain's stooge in the Pole?

"Ha!

"A) I'm not interested one snowflake in taking my father's place, and

"B) there's doubly no way in summer that I'd do it as Samhain's lackey.

"Once was enough. No thanks!

"I'll find Talbot, but only to help Pop. *You hear what I'm caroling?*"

The Count throws back his head and gives his malevolent, trademark laugh.

"What's so funny?" I demand.

After a few moments, the Count wipes his eyes, his laughter settling.

"It's just that you try so hard not to be what you so obviously are. It's quite amusing!" With that, he breaks into laughter once more.

I feel like breaking his face!

I take a step forward, intending to do just that when I look around the room and realize what the Count was laughing about.

The walls, ceiling, and floor are covered with frost and, despite the doors and windows being closed, the wind is blowing furiously around us.

I look at Lenny. He's hugging himself, his teeth chattering beneath the icicle hanging from his nose.

He's scared.

Of me.

I'm doing this. Without realizing it. My temper has gotten out of control and with it, so have my powers. I'm throwing the same kind of blizzard tantrums the Old Man is infamous for. I feel disgusted with myself.

I stow the picture in my pocket and then turn and exit the room, slamming the door behind me, the Count's laughter echoing in my ears.

Jack woke to find that he lay on a couch.
He rubbed his head and it hurt. "Ow! Ouch!"
"Hello, Jack," the vampire said. "Ve're glad you're avake."
"Right," Jack said. "But I have no blood for you to take!"

"Please, Jack. Listen. Ve just vant to speak.
"It's in our best interests you find who you seek.
"How can I trust you?" Is what Jack said.
"After all, it was you who bonked me on the head!"

"That was me, Jack," said Lenny Frankensteinbeck.
"It wasn't my intention to your skull wreck."
"Okay," Jack said, "Come on. Spit it out!
"Tell me right now what this is all about!"

The vampire spoke up. "Ve can give you the perp's name.
"It vas a verevolf called Talbot who is to blame.
"Ve think he's hiding out in Valentine Land.
"If you'd go get him, it sure vould be grand!"

Jack was suspicious. "What do you get out of this?"
"All the trick or treating ve'll othervise miss.
"How many kids can a vampire give fright,
"Vith them asleep in their beds for the long silent night?"

CHAPTER 12

Flash is there waiting for me when I get back to H-Town. We zoom across the night sky for the aurora borealis. In no time, I'm back at the Pole with Fred running a background check on Lupercalia Lovelace. Fred runs it off the 'grid.' The grid is part of something he calls the 'enter-net,' though he never enters a net or anything else. So far as I can tell, he just sits at his computer.

"Yo!" Fred calls when he finds the info. "Lupercalia Lovelace. A nymph from the house of Juno. She's got a few misdemeanors, but nothing serious.

"She's the owner-operator of the Siren's Song. It's a popular watering hole Valentine side. Loveland to be exact."

Fred swivels his chair away from his computer to face me. "Shouldn't be too hard to find, J-Dog."

"Thanks, Fred. You got a secure line I can make calls from?"

"Word. The globe in my bedroom. It's tricked with the latest anti-spyware. Should be safe enough."

I go to Fred's bedroom and put in a call to the castle. A Blond-headed elf with a dentist's coat appears within the crystal ball.

"Hello?" he says.

"Sherman, it's Jack."

"Oh. Hi, Jack."

"Mom around?"

"She's sleeping. You want me to wake her?"

"Nah. That's okay. She needs her rest right now. When she wakes, tell her I called. Tell her I said—"

"Yeah, Jack?"

"Tell her I said I'm getting close."

"Okay, Jack."

I hang up and put in a call to Dee's office.

"Hello?" Her voice comes through but not her image.

"Call me at this number from a pay-palantir in five minutes. Voice only."

I hang up and wait. Five minutes later, the globe jingles on cue.

"Jack?"

"It's me, Dee."

"Are you back? Why the cloak and dagger routine?"

"I found him, Dee. I found our wolf Halloween side. He's a lowlife named Larry Talbot."

"You did? Where is he? What did he say?"

"He got away before I could snowstorm him, Dee. But listen, *he was waiting on me.*"

"Oh no! Are you okay?"

"I'm fine, Dee. But you see, he knew I was coming. Did you tell anyone I was going Halloween side?"

"No. No one. What are you saying, Jack?"

"I'm saying it was a trap. And he said he was following orders. And it doesn't look like they were from Samhain.

"Dee, I think this is bigger than either of us suspected. I think this is about more than just some rogue Holiday world trying to raise its status above Christmas."

"You think there's someone inside City Hall."

I nod, though Dee's not around to see it. "I always said you were one sharp ice skate."

"What are you going to do?"

"I've got no proof—yet. Finding Talbot will be the best way to finger whoever's behind all this."

"Where are you going to look for him?"

"It's best I don't say. Even over this line. You never know who could be listening in.

"I'll call you when I get back. In the meantime, keep an eye out around the office. If you notice anyone acting suspicious, keep tabs on them. Don't act! Just watch. Don't put yourself in harm's way under any circumstances. Okay?"

"But, Jack I—"

"*Promise me, Dee.* I couldn't take losing both Pop and you on the same watch. Promise me."

"I—I promise, Jack."

"I'll talk to you, soon." I hang up and bid Fred goodbye.

Before you can blink, Flash and I are out of the Pole and over Holiday Town flying toward its amusement park. It's the off season, not to mention late at night, so the park will be closed—*not that it matters to me either way.*

We reach the park and I leave Flash behind as I jump the gate. The park is deserted—not even a wandering security guard to be seen. I bypass Ferris wheels and roller coasters, heading deeper inside until I reach the Tunnel of Love built over the park's lake.

I help myself to a boat and steer it inside the tunnel. As I float down the tube, conveniently dark for young lovers, I can't help but think of all the times Dee and I took our own boat rides here.

Ah, sweet memories.

Finally, I come out the tunnel's other side and begin to ascend the track that will ultimately drop the boat into splashdown. I crest the ramp's apex and concentrate on my feelings for Dee.

Thinking about something you cherish—*or even love*—is necessary to journey to Valentine side. Otherwise, you just finish the ride in the park, ending up soaking wet!

The boat descends the ramp like a torpedo moving at high velocity. The boat hits the water and plummets beneath the surface. The next thing I know, my head is bobbing in the water just off the Loveland shore.

The trip always amuses me. I guess love does feel a lot like you're drowning in some ways.

I swim to shore. It may be night, but here in Loveland, it's always springtime.

I am immediately unhappy.

Spring is too close to summer for my liking. I prefer to stay where just above freezing is considered a scorcher, thank you very much!

I make my way inland. There's no need to dry off. The water freezes right to me, fitting in naturally with my already frosty exterior.

Soon, I hit downtown and, as is the usual here, attractive

young godlings hold hands and trade love notes as they walk down either side of the street. Chubby cupids and winged, anthropomorphic hearts flitter above their heads, losing arrows of love left and right.

Sometimes even I think the Pole is a bit much with its candy cane road signs and sugar cookie manhole covers. But it's got nothing on the sappy, greeting card billboards and chocolate-covered lampposts here in Loveland. The whole town is sickeningly sweet to the last sprite, nymph, and cupid. I can't half blame the Count for not wanting to set foot here.

I shake my head and venture farther down the street. A flying cupid decides to use me for target practice. Without pausing in stride, I freeze the arrow just as he loses it from his bow. It falls and hits the ground, shattering into a satisfyingly large number of pieces.

The cupid starts to notch another arrow, but I give him the briefest glance with the Eye and it sends him fluttering off in the other direction.

It isn't long before I reach the Siren's Song. It's a wine and dessert bar with a spiraling staircase in the back leading to an upper floor. The place is deserted except for a blonde girl tidyng up, her back turned to me.

"We're closed," she calls without looking at me. "Come back later."

"That's alright," I say, striding toward her. "I'm not here for refreshments."

"Then what," she says as she turns toward me, "exactly, are you here...well, well! Aren't you a handsome devil?"

If she's taken with me, it's not half as much as I am with her. The Count's photograph did not even begin to do Luprecalia justice. It's her standing before me and she is an absolute knock-out! Golden-haired and blue-eyed with bronze skin, her beauty is at the opposite end of the spectrum from Dee's, but it's every bit as striking.

I try to shake it off and play it cool. It works, more or less.

"Lupercalia Lovelace?"

She closes the distance between us and raises her hand in greeting. I take it in mine. Her skin feels as soft as a baby's.

"Honey," she says, ogling me with her eyes, "you may call me whatever you want."

"I'm Frost."

I release her hand and take a few steps back, pretending like I'm surveying the room so that she doesn't realize the gesture for what it really is—*a retreat.*

"Don't they have first names where you come from?" she teases.

"*Frost,*" I say with finality.

"You're one cool customer, Frost," she says, still teasing.

"Nice place you have here," I say.

She closes the gap between us once more, purposely invading my space. Suddenly, it feels like summer in here.

"It pays the bills," she says. "How about one on the house?"

"Pardon me?"

"A drink. We're closed, so it would be on me."

"Eggnog," I say, relieved to have an excuse to get her away from me, "heavy on the nog."

"I'll see what I can do."

She disappears into a back room and I breathe a heavy sigh of relief. A moment later, she comes back holding a tall decanter and two slim, jeweled goblets.

"I'm afraid all I have is dessert wine."

I nod. She sits down at a table, motioning me for me to join her. I do so, reluctantly. At least the table will be between us.

"So," she says as she pours us both a glass, "what *does* bring you to the Siren's Song?"

"Your boyfriend." I say matter-of-factly.

"I'm afraid I don't follow you." She bats her eyelids invitingly. "*I'm perfectly, wonderfully single.*"

I take a drink of the wine. It's warm and melts the frost in my throat.

"Larry Talbot."

She straightens in her seat at the mention of his name.

"Ah, yes. Larry. What has he done now? Stolen something like he stole my heart?"

"Kidnapping."

She looks shocked. "You don't say? I knew he was a bad

apple, in the fun kind of way. But I never dreamed he was capable of kidnapping someone!"

She throws up her hands. "Not that I'm surprised. I always did have a weakness for men with an edge."

She leans in so close I can smell her perfume. It's like roses and it leaves me spellbound.

"Maybe that's why I'm finding myself liking you so much."

I lean in. "Lupercalia?"

She leans in so close our noses almost touch. "Yeah?"

"Where is he?"

"Who?"

"Where's—?"

I snap straight in my chair as a loud thump sounds from upstairs. One look into her guilty eyes tells me I've been snow jobbed!

Lupercalia's fancy with me is all an act to keep me busy—occupied so Larry can make a run for it. I'd like to give her a piece of my mind, but I don't have time.

I bolt for the stairs and then take them two at a time. I kick open the first door I come to in time to see Larry's tail disappearing out a window. I run into the room and step over the lamp his tail must have accidentally knocked to the floor as he was making his escape. Its fall must have been what we heard below.

I duck my head out the window and see Larry leaping gracefully to the street a full three stories below. I curse and then fling myself through the window.

The wind whistles in my ears for a moment and then I'm falling through the goo of a marshmallow-bus stop. The few godlings waiting for a ride look on at me wide-mouthed in surprise. I must look ridiculous, covered in marshmallow goo, but I don't have time to worry about that. Larry is getting away!

He lopes down the street, frightened nymphs and cupids scattering before him. He's heading for the shore. I've got to catch him before he reaches the water and escapes back to H-Town.

It's too hot for ice magic, so I snatch a bow and quiver of arrows from one of the cupids Larry unsettled. The cupid regains his senses and starts shouting for the police, but he's too late. I'm already two blocks away.

I knock an arrow and fire in mid-run. It goes wide. Larry's almost to the shore. I have to make this one count. I draw another arrow and shoot. It misses Larry by inches. He swerves, realizing he's under fire.

Larry's at the beach now. Time has almost run out. I stop in the middle of the road and knock an arrow. I draw back the bow, blocking out the terrain, the honking horns, the nervous yells of the onlookers. I exhale, zeroing in on Larry.

Then I fire.

The arrow whistles away and strikes home in the back of Larry's leg. His leg goes all rubbery, full of soft, warm emotion. It doesn't stop him, but slows him down enough that I should be able to catch him easily.

Then, before I realize what's happening, I feel my arms being yanked behind me so that candied handcuffs can slap over my wrists.

"Hey? What the—?"

"You have the right to remain silent," one of the police-sprites taking me into custody says over the buzz of his heart-shaped walkie-talkie, "If you choose to give up that right—!"

I look back down the beach and see the tip of Larry's tail disappear beneath the waves.

"No! No! No!" I plead, "You're letting him get away!"

"Oh, don't worry," one of the other police-sprites says. "We've got our man, alright!"

"—Nutcrackers!"

To the North Pole to see his pal Fred,
Is where Private Eye Jack Frost then fled.
He badly needed a solid lead,
To on the werewolf Talbot, get a bead.

"We can track him down," Fred said, "I'll just bet,
"Doing a search on the internet.
"Ah, now we have him. Oh yeah, here we are.
"It appears his girlfriend runs a wine bar."

"I'll pay her a visit," Jack said, "See if Talbot's there.
"With me looking for him, he can't hide anywhere.
At the H-Town Fun Park, Jack took a ride,
Down the Tunnel of Love to Valentine-side.

He met Talbot's girl. Her name was Lovelace.
She was a looker, full of poise and grace.
But her seductive exterior was all just a sham.
Talbot was there lying low, hiding, on the lam.

Through the streets, Jack gave chase,
Pursuing Talbot in a speedy foot race!
With a cupid's bow and arrow, he slowed the wolf down.
But then the Valentine police tackled Jack to the ground!

CHAPTER 13

"I love you, man!"

I roll my eyes and slide down the bench, trying to put as much space between me and the Dionysian godling confessing his feelings for me. He just as quickly closes the gap, this time putting an arm around my shoulder.

I try not to get too angry with him as he's riddled full of police-issue cupid arrows and therefore can't help himself.

But it does little good.

"No, really," he says, "*I. Love. You. Man!*"

"Oh yeah? Well, love me from over there!" I tell him, having little choice but to give him a bit of the Eye. It snaps him to his senses and he goes scurrying to the other side of our jail cell. "Hmph," I snort, "Imprisoned behind bars of steel-hard chocolate. How embarrassing."

"Frost!"

My other cellmates glance at me as the guard calls my name.

"Front and center. You have a visitor."

In a small act of rebellion, I make them wait a second. Then I slowly get up and walk to the jail cell entrance. The guard opens the door and escorts me down the bubblegum-pink hallway to a series of gumdrop-covered booths. Dee sits on the booths' other side, patiently awaiting me. I take at a seat at one and she joins me. Through the window separating us, I see she's holding a bouquet of roses.

"For me?" I ask. It takes her a second to realize I'm talking about the rose bouquet in her hand.

"These? Since I've arrived here, I've been given at least a dozen every time I walk into a new room. But a girl knows never to turn down roses. You should've bought me more!"

"Would it have made a difference?"

"Maybe."

"Story of my life."

"What happened, Jack? How did you get inside here?"

"I went to see Talbot's girlfriend—"

"This Lupercalia you mentioned over the globe? Should I be jealous?"

"Hush. You know better than that. I went to see her and found our wolf hiding upstairs. He ran. I made chase."

"We'll send some feds out to pick her up."

"Make sure they're female."

"Why?"

"No reason."

"So? How does a friendly visit land you in the big house?"

"—Talbot was getting away. I had to do the *gift swap* with a cupid for his bow and arrow. Put one in Talbot's leg. The cops nabbed me for theft before I could collar him."

"Where did Talbot go?"

"H-Town. You two probably passed each other on your way over."

"*Hardy-har-har.* I talked to Father Time when you called. He's pulling what strings he can, but this falls under Loveland jurisdiction."

"Where does that leave me?"

"I'm afraid you're going to have to sit tight until he can get those favors called in. Shouldn't be longer than a century or two."

"*And me without my toothbrush.*"

"These things take time, Jack."

"Well, time we've got. An eternity's worth unless I can get out of here and get to finding Pop!"

"Time's up," the guard warns from behind me. It's unclear to me if he's trying to be ironic.

"I've got to go, Jack," Dee says as she stands. "I'll keep on his Honor. We'll have you out of here soon. You'll see."

"Yeah."

"Bye, Jack."

I watch Dee leave and then return to my cell.

I'm behind bars while the holidayers who kidnapped my father are running free as a reindeer in wintertime. I'm about as low as an elemental can get.

I try to think about what Pop would do in a situation like this. He would've had everyone hugging and singing Christmas carols by now—probably have the prisoners begging to serve his sentence for him and the guards falling over themselves to let him go. The man's just that way—spreads good cheer wherever he goes. To know him, is to love him. I speak from experience.

And that troubles me all the more. I'm half-surprised the jolly fat fellow hasn't popped up again all on his own, his captor reformed, apologetic, and ready to turn himself in. Whomever is behind all this is one cold-hearted criminal, even by my standards.

Suddenly, thinking about all this, I'm terrified for Pop—of where he is, of what's being done to him. I'm just about to jump out of my seat and scream and beat the cell bars until they let me out of here when the *Christmas Angel* speaks from beside me.

"I wouldn't do that, if I were you, Jack."

"Hello, *Epiphany*," I say, trying to play it cool. It always rattles me when she just *appears* like this. "Haven't seen you around in millennia."

"I'm a busy celestial." Epiphany folds her white-robed arms. She's pretty hum-drum by angel standards. No wings or halos. Not even a heavenly glow.

"I can imagine. So, since you're talking to me and no one else here seems to notice you, can I assume you've come to bring *the walls tumblin' down*?"

Epiphany chuckles. Her laughter is melodious.

"No, I'm afraid—"

Epiphany notices a prisoner crying in the corner—a Mexican Independence Day revolutionary. She gets up and walks over to him, though he remains oblivious to her presence. She bends down and cups her hand to whisper something into his ear. Immediately his tears dry up and a look of peace spreads over his face.

Moments later, she's sitting beside me once again. "Now, as

I was saying—I'm afraid that, in these modern times, we prefer not to interfere with natural law, *or even supernatural law,* when possible. A more indirect approach seems to work best for all concerned."

"Well, ain't that just holly jolly for me?"

"Don't fret, Jack. I didn't say I was going to leave you totally without support."

"If by support you mean anything other than a lock pick, then it's nutcrackers to me."

"Oh, Jack. So glum. Perhaps you just need to take a closer look at what tools you already have available."

"Tools? I could freeze those bars all I wanted and it wouldn't do any good. They're magically reinforced. And you wouldn't know it to look at them, but those guards are too strong-willed for the Eye. Believe me. I tried. I'm lucky they left me in here with the clothes on my—!"

I turn to look Epiphany directly in the eye, but she's already gone, her work here done.

What an idiot I am! The guards left me my clothes, specifically my stocking-fedora and trench-cloak. Now, if I can just somehow trick the guards into opening the door, I can go dim and slip out of here!

I stand up and sigh, knowing what I must do. I pick out the biggest, meanest-looking prisoner I can find—a man-sized groundhog standing upright on its hind-legs. I waltz up to him.

"What are you looking at?" I ask, bowing my chest out at him.

He ignores me and continues swinging his head nervously from side-to-side, eyeing the floor.

"I said, what are you looking—?"

"Please tell me you haven't seen it!" He says without taking his eyes off the floor.

"Seen what?"

"My shadow. I had them lock me up to get away from it, but it's tricky! I always have to be on the lookout."

I turn away, realizing that I'm not going to get anywhere with this 'fraidy-cat. Then inspiration strikes and I turn back.

"Great Santa's beard!" I say pointing at the groundhog's clawed feet. "There it is!"

It works better than I could've possibly hoped. The ground-hog doesn't even wait to ask if I'm talking about his shadow. He simply bolts in terror, climbing over our fellow prisoners for the other side of the room and doing a wonderful job of riling them up in the process. The next thing I know, there's a full-scale brawl going on inside the jail cell.

I back into a corner and go dim as guards in full riot gear come charging into the cell, cupid bows strung behind heart-shaped shields. I let them pass and slip out unnoticed.

Two shakes of a snow globe later, I'm off shore and swimming for H-Town.

Jack Frost sat in jail, trying to think.
"I can't believe I'm here, on ice, in the clink!"
"Frost, you have a visitor," the prison guard said.
Then down the hallway, Jack Frost he led.

Dee sat waiting at a visitation booth.
"We're trying to free you, Jack. I swear it's the truth!
"Father Time's on it. He'll call in a favor.
"He'll have you of here, sooner or later.

"It may take a millennium or more,
"But time we have, centuries galore!"
Jack returned to his cell, feeling very sick.
He needed to get out of here and free Saint Nick!"

That's when the Christmas Angel before Jack appeared.
Her reputation among the elves was highly revered.
"Tell me, please," Jack said, "Are you here to spring me?"
"Free thy self," the angel said, "the means is with thee."

The angel was gone as quick as she spoke.
But right then Jack remembered his concealing trench-cloak.
He caused a ruckus and the guards opened his cell door.
Then he slipped away to leave Loveland's shore.

CHAPTER 14

"J!" Fred says, shocked to see me when he opens his front door.

"It ain't exactly safe for me out here in the night, Fred."

"Yo," Fred says, stepping back to let me inside, "Mi casa, su casa, homie."

I enter and collapse on Fred's couch, exhausted from all the *duck and cover* on the way back to the Pole. Traveling on Flash wouldn't have been exactly low key, after all.

Fred shuts the door behind us.

"What in Cringle's name have you been up to, J? Your mugshot's everywhere. Even the feds are looking for you!"

Great. Now even the feds are gunning for me. How could I Scrooge up this case any worse?

"There was a *misunderstanding* back in Loveland. I'll square it up soon enough. But that's not the worst news."

"Yo?"

"Our wolf got away, Fred. The trail's cold. *Cold as ice.*"

"What can I do to help?"

I grin at him. "I was hoping you'd say that. I need you to run a list of Talbot's known associates. Cross reference that with those of a Ms. Lupercalia Lovelace, then give me what you come up with."

"It could take a while, J. H-Town's tightening their e-security with everything that's been going down."

"Can you crack it?"

"*What's my name, yo?*"

"Good elf. Mind if I grab some shuteye here while I wait? I'm beat."

"Word."

Fred leaves for his workshop and I lie back and put my hat down over my eyes. Despite my weariness, I can't fall asleep. My thoughts won't allow me. I give up trying and take a crack at wrapping my brain around this case.

Who benefits? That's the question here and it's one that keeps coming up with too many answers. Despite what they say, the Old Man, and through the Count, Samhain, both have reasons to want Santa on ice for good.

The Old Man no longer has anyone keeping him in check at the Pole, and Samhain and his crew may now move among the realms as they please, no daylight to hold them back. But neither suspect feels right.

If nothing else, the elf unions would organize the minute they were certain Pop would no longer be running the show. That would give the Old Man headaches without end!

And, like the Count said, Samhain's folk might simply wither away without a steady supply of tricks-or-treats coming through.

Yet, this case has both their fingerprints all over it—the snowstorm that *oh so conveniently* covered the actual kidnapping had to have been brewed by the Old Man.

And it's no coincidence it was Talbot, a Halloweenian, who tried to ice Father Time.

Why would either boss involve themselves in something so detrimental to their respective *businesses*?

It had to be because they had no choice.

Someone or something had to have forced their hands—someone or something they didn't dare say no to. But who or what could have such power over two such formidable beings? It is with this question gnawing away at my mind that sleep finally overtakes me.

"Yo!" Fred says as he shakes me awake. "Wake up, J! Wake up!"

"Leave me alone," I say, rolling over. "I just got to sleep!"

"You've been out for hours, J! But you got to bounce, yo! The feds are here!"

I'm wide awake at his words. I spring to my feet, realizing

the drumming noise in the dream I was having is really the feds pounding on Fred's door.

"Why didn't you wake me?"

"I tried. But never mind! Here!" Fred shoves a printout into my hands. "It's a list of the perps you wanted. Now get the holly out of here!"

I go dim and sprint for the back door. I pull up short when I see through the windows that the place is surrounded.

"Nutcrackers!"

I head back down the hallway and then freeze when I hear Fred on the losing end of an argument with someone in the living room.

"You have no right!" Fred yells.

"Rights are not our concern," the other voice says. "We have a job to do!"

"I won't have it!"

"Enough. Take him into custody."

"You can't do this! You can't—!" But then Fred is gone. The voice's next words chill my already frozen bones.

"Bring in the Cerberus."

"Nutcrackers!"

I bolt down the hallway for the stairs, heading up to Fred's bedroom. Being dim won't hide me from any three-headed police dog. I've got to get out of here and fast!

I slowly open Fred's bedroom window, praying no one outside will notice.

Someone *upstairs* must be listening. The feds and the blue caps with them keep their eyes glued on the backdoor.

I climb out into the night air and, as carefully and quietly as possible, shimmy down a candy-cane gutter. I hang just above the ground, not knowing how I'm going to get down without them seeing my tracks in the snow.

Fred unknowingly resolves this problem for me, too. He comes around the corner in cuffs, escorted by two feds, about to be stuffed into a patrol-sleigh. He catches them off guard and slips out of their hands to make a break for it. The feds and blue caps standing around leave to assist their fellow officers in his recapture.

Good ol' Fred.

I get down and form an ice-jimmy to unlock one of the patrol-sleighs. Thanks to the days of my youth Halloween side, it's as easy to do as falling off a Yule log.

I consider jacking the sleigh, but dismiss the notion as doing so would only bring the feds down on me that much faster. Instead, a much more advantageous option catches my eye—a small canvas bag closed with a draw string.

I turn visible and snatch the bag up. I open it and dump the glistening dust held inside over my head just as the feds come back with a very mussed Fred in tow.

"Lieutenant," one of the feds says, his voice full of surprise. "I didn't know you were on this assignment."

The dust I'm now covered in is a *glamour,* one often used by undercover cops. It's magic that makes anyone looking at you see someone else—someone who wouldn't be out of place.

Sometimes, like now, being visible, but incognito, has its advantages over dimness. Still, it won't fool the Cerberus, so I have to get out of here asap!

"City Hall sent me over. Special orders from the mayor. I'm to escort this man back to H-Town on the double."

"Sure. But regulations say I need to call it in to confirm."

"Don't throw the reg book at me, Sergeant! I know it backward and forward. His Honor would be very displeased if he heard you were delaying his orders.

"But go ahead! Act like a rookie who can't put his pants on without permission from downtown if you have to."

I hold my breath while the sergeant considers. I breath a deep sigh of relief when he gives in.

"Forgive me. By all means, take him away."

He gives an inch but, being me, I take a mile. *"Take him away, what?"*

"Take him away, sir. That is, forgive me, sir."

He passes Fred over to me.

"You're forgiven, Sergeant. Now call in as soon as you have that no-good Frost in custody."

"Sir, yes, sir!" he says, snapping off a salute.

I make it look as though I'm circling around front with Fred.

Just as soon as we're out of eyeshot from either side of the house, I uncuff him using the jimmy.

"That was close, Yo."

"How'd you know it was me?"

"He saw a fed. I saw Alfie. Figured you'd jacked a glamour."

"You figured right."

"What now, J?"

"Now we get out of here. Thanks to you, I've got leads to follow. Anywhere safe you can lay low for a while?"

"I've been meaning to visit my cousin in the Antarctic. He's got an awesome crib, yo! And the honeys southside, woo!"

"Probably best until I can get all this snow shoveled."

Fred gives me an awkward hip-hop-hug. I reluctantly return it.

"Guess it's goodbye, then," he says. "Yo, good luck finding your Pop, J."

"Thanks. If what's happened so far is any indication, *I'm going to need it.*"

Back at the Pole, Jack knocked on Fred's door.
"Let me in, Fred. It's not safe anymore!"
"Yo, J! Are you crazy? Get your butt inside!
"Your face is on the news. You need to hide!"

"Tell me, J," Fred said, "I don't understand.
"How exactly did you become a wanted man?"
"I'm afraid," Jack said, "there's been a misunderstanding.
"For a crime I didn't commit, me they are branding."

"I need to rest, Fred. May I crash on your couch?"
"Make yourself at home, J. My crib ain't no slouch."
But sleep wouldn't' come, so the crime Jack pondered.
Who kidnapped my pop? Over this question his mind wandered.

Could it be Talbot, the Old Man, or the Halloween folk?
I've got to figure this out, and that ain't no joke!
Just when Jack had finally closed his eyes,
The police came a' knocking, much to his surprise!

"Come out, Frost!" the cops said. "We know you're inside!"
"J, you gotta bounce!" Fred said. "You must run and hide!"
"I know," Jack said. "I'll go in disguise by magical means.
"I'll use a glamour so my true face can't be seen."

CHAPTER 15

It takes a little longer to navigate the aurora borealis without Flash, but I make it to H-Town just fine on my own.

Next, I set about the task of finding a rainbow in the night sky. Impossible to have a rainbow at night? Not in H-Town. There's always a rainbow leading out of the city somewhere. It's just a matter of knowing how to find it.

Good thing I'm a detective.

Who benefits? Another way of phrasing that question is to ask, "Where does the money lead?"

And when it comes to bankrolling a kidnapping on the scale of Pop's, no Holiday folk would be more equipped to do so than the leprechauns of the St. Patrick's Day realm—especially a certain leprechaun named Mickey O'Shaunessey, an infamous money launderer who just so happens to be at the top of the list of Larry Talbot's known associates. And since it's a leprechaun I'm hunting for, then a rainbow I'll need.

I rummage in a city trash can until I find a clear glass bottle. Still bent over the can, I feel someone tap me on the back of my shoulder. I rise up and gasp to see a fed leering down at me.

"Move it along, you," he says. "Get down to the homeless shelter with the rest of the rabble. They'll feed you and give you a place to sleep."

I sigh with relief. The glamour is still working. When the fed saw someone rummaging in the garbage, he expected it to be a transient, so that's who he sees.

"Yes sir, officer," I reply as I hide the bottle behind my back. "Certainly."

I walk down the rain-puddled street, putting distance

between myself and the fed. When I'm out of eye-shot, I duck down a graffiti-covered alleyway that has the last of the three things I need to come up with a rainbow.

I take the bottle and dip it into a rain puddle, letting it fill half full. Then I hold it out and tilt it back and forth, allowing the light from one of the lamps along the outer street to play against the bottle's surface.

In no time, a small scale prism effect occurs between the light, the bottle, and the water inside it. The effect builds and becomes self-sustaining until before I know it, there's a full-sized rainbow arcing up from the alley floor into the night sky above.

"Saints' begorrah," I say with a wry smile. Then I begin walking up the rainbow.

What seems like hours later, the rainbow forks. One branch of it rises even higher to the Norse god realm of Asgard. I know this because there's a kaleidoscopic road sign sticking out of the rainbow saying so.

The other branch bends earthward. I double check the road sign and, sure enough, it labels the downward branch as the route to the Emerald Isle. That's the one I want.

I start down it and, before long, I can see its end at a small island of rolling green hills amid a sea of crashing waves. Once on the island, I walk inland until I come to a modest stone tavern with a thatched roof. Young leprechauns in green frock coats and bowler hats stand outside, eyeing me wearily over their pints of ale.

"I'm here to see Mickey," I say.

"Well, Mickey's not taking visitors today," one of the leprechaun's says, his Irish brogue high and thick. "Try your luck tomorrow."

The other leprechauns laugh and toast.

"He'll want to see me," I say.

The laughter halts immediately.

The talker puts down his pint and gets in my face, obviously not pleased I didn't walk away when I had the chance.

"And just why would Mickey want to see you?" he asks.

"That's for Mickey to know," I say. "But you can tell him a

friend of Larry Talbot's has come to call."

The talker's eyes narrow at the mention of Talbot's name. Without another word, he turns and goes into the tavern. A minute later, he reappears and motions for me to join him inside.

I feel the other leprechauns sizing me up as I pass them by and head into the tavern. They're spoiling for one of the only five things a leprechaun cares about. Of the five, it's the one I hate the most.

The tavern is deserted save for the talker, a barkeep, and one older leprechaun sitting by himself at a table in the far corner.

He motions me over. "Come! Sit."

I do.

The older leprechaun is dressed in a green frock coat and bowler hat like the others. His face is wrinkled and his red side-burns are threaded with gray. He twiddles a pipe between his teeth. One of them is capped with brilliant gold. He's short like the others, but thick and burly, with a mischievous gleam in his eye.

He reminds me of a leprechaun who visited the Pole once when I was a boy. He helped himself to our eggnog and got *squirrely*. It took ten of Alfie's blue caps to bring him down and every one of them was black and blue when it was all over.

I wonder who the glamour makes him see me as. Probably a Halloweenian as I came asking for Talbot.

"Drink?" he asks, his brogue so deep and thick that it takes me a minute to realize I'm being offered refreshment.

"Egg—uh—blood wine?"

"Horrid stuff." He gestures to the bar keep. "Bring us a pint."

The leprechaun shifts in his seat and empties the tobacco from his pipe.

"So, lad. It appears you have me at a disadvantage. You know my name, but I'm afraid I don't know yours."

"Call me Larry. Like your friend. Have you seen Talbot lately?"

The barkeep sits the drinks down between us.

"Not one to beat around the bush, are ye?" the leprechaun, now revealed as Mickey, says.

"I don't have the luxury of small talk, right now."

"Oh lad, pleasant conversation in the company of others is not a luxury, but an Irishman's right. But, have it your way."

"Is Talbot here?"

He drinks a long swig of ale and then wipes the foam from his chin.

"Do ye like riddles, lad?"

"I like them solved."

"Good, good. I'll tell ye what: I'll answer your question if ye can answer one of mine. But fail in the answering and ye become my servant for a century."

Great. Dealing with fairies, I've always dreaded being put in a position where I have to make this kind of cornball choice. But I never thought I'd actually have to. Live and Learn.

"I really don't have time for games and riddles."

"Take it or leave it, laddie."

I sigh. "Alright. Shoot."

He grins, pleased to no end. "Riddle me this," he says:

I never was, am always to be,
No one ever saw me, nor ever will,
And yet I am the confidence of all
Who live and breathe on this terrestrial ball!

Nutcrackers. I don't have a clue. Give me facts to solve a case, not some silly word-play.

Frustrated, I mumble under my breath. "If I don't solve this and find Pop, there's not going to be a tomorrow ever again."

Suddenly, Mickey slams the pint of ale he'd been holding to his mouth down on the table.

"Well played, lad," he says, "and solved in no time at all. Tell me, what exactly was it that tipped ye off to *tomorrow* being the answer?"

My eyes briefly widen with realization.

"Uh," I say, fumbling for an answer, "that old riddle? Everyone knows that. But I've done what you asked. Now answer my question."

Mickey sighs deeply. "Very well. I believe the question you asked was, 'is Talbot here?' "

Mickey leans back and crosses his arms, a smug smile spreading over his face. "Aye. He was, lad. But not anymore!" Mickey leans forward and slaps the table as he guffaws with laughter."

"Where did he go?" I ask.

"Oh!" Mickey says, his eyes refilling with excitement. "That's another question ye want answered lad. One that will be costing ye!"

I roll my eyes. "Another riddle then?"

"No, no, lad," Mickey says, shaking his head. "Truth be told I'm no fan of riddles, me self. They hurt me head!"

"But I am of faerie after all, and so felt obligated to at least take a pass at such where ye was concerned."

Mickey takes off his jacket and begins rolling up his sleeves, the gleam in his eye growing, his pipe dancing between his teeth.

"For ye next test, I had something a bit more *hands on* in mind."

I don't like the sound of this and I'm right not to.

Remember that one of five things I mentioned leprechauns love for that I hate—the thing the younger ones were spoiling for? Apparently, Mickey is spoiling for it, too.

Moments later, he and I are out front circling one another, our *dukes* up, the other leprechauns surrounding us, booing me and cheering for him.

"Rules?" he asks.

"Uh," I say, "no magic?"

With no harsh winter to pull from, I wouldn't stand a chance against him in a magical battle here on his home turf.

Mickey grins. "Wouldn't have it any other way, lad!"

He stomps my foot and serves me three quick knuckle sandwiches before I even know what's on the menu.

He releases my foot and I go stumbling backward into a mass of shouting leprechauns. They just as quickly shove me back toward Mickey.

I duck just in time to miss a haymaker and manage to connect with one of my own that leaves Mickey dazed.

He shakes it off and smiles from ear to ear, as happy as I've ever seen anyone.

Did I mention that leprechauns are insane?

To describe the rest of the fight would be pointless other than to say we both fought long and hard.

When at last I wake up, I see Mickey smiling as he stands over me, one eye blackened and his gold tooth missing, his hand held out to lift me up.

"Laddie, that was the most fun I've had in centuries!" Mickey says as he helps me to my feet. "A finer bout of fisticuffs, I cannot remember."

"Yeah," I say, wincing in pain. *"Big fun."*

It hurts to talk. In fact, at the moment, it hurts to do anything. I struggle, but manage to raise my fists.

"Well, come on. Let's go. Round two."

Mickey and the other leprechauns guffaw as he jovially slaps my shoulder.

"We'll make a leprechaun out of ye yet! But no, lad, it's over."

"Not until you tell me where Talbot went to. Not by a long shot."

"Easy, lad. Relax. The object wasn't to beat me. No one can do that! Not here on the Emerald Isle. You just had to take me for a dance and show me a good time, and that you did and more."

I lower my fists as Mickey puts his arm around my shoulder.

"I'll be happy to tell a fighting man like yourself where that no-good wolf got to," he says. "Twas me who sent him packing there in the first place, and good riddance to him!"

I sigh with relief. If we'd gone another round, there would've only been two more hits: Mickey hitting me and then me hitting the ground. For good.

"Where did you send him, Mickey?"

He grins at the other leprechauns, preparing them for the joke about to leave his mouth.

"Well, it so happens, Mr. Talbot owes me a large sum of money. It also just so happens, he's had some, shall we say, *unseemly dealings* with the Cottontails that didn't leave him on the best of terms with them.

"In fact, the Cottontails were so terribly out of sorts about it, they offered a hefty sum of gold for anyone who could, shall we say, *reconnect* them with Mr. Talbot."

Mickey grins, ready to drop the joke.

"Now, there's nothing more than a leprechaun likes than gold. And wouldn't you know it? By the luck of the Irish, the sum of money the Cottontails were offering was equal to and beyond what our Mr. Talbot owed yours truly.

"So, when Talbot had the nerve to ask for sanctuary when still unable to pay off his debt, there was only one viable option left to me."

Mickey puts his fingers to his bowler hat, mimicking bunny ears as he begins hopping around.

Did I mention leprechauns are insane?

"Here comes Peter Cottontail," he sings, "Hopping down on Talbot's tail. Hippity-hoppity, Talbot's taken away!"

The leprechauns slap their knees and let loose with gut-busting laughter. I'd find it funny, too, if not for the fact that the Cottontails are the most vicious, brutal gang in all the Holiday worlds and I was about to have to walk smack down in the middle of them.

Jack set out for the Emerald Isle.
There was a leprechaun there who was high profile.
"Being on the run ain't cheap. Talbot will need dough."
"So to the leprechaun, the werewolf might go."

Jack traveled between worlds over the rainbow bridge.
Soon the Isle came into view, just over the ridge.
To a small stone tavern, Jack Frost came.
For there resided Mickey, a leprechaun of great fame.

Thanks to the glamour's magic, he couldn't see Jack's face.
Just as well, Jack thought. Disguise is best in this case.
"I'll ask you a riddle," Mickey said, "Best answer it true.
"Or you'll be my servant, until time runs anew!"

For the riddle's answer, Jack floundered and fumbled,
But his luck held, and upon it he stumbled.
"Fair enough," Mickey said, "your answer was right.
"But to learn Talbot's whereabouts, me you must fight!"

Through house and yard, they rocked and rolled,
But at last the leprechaun came up silver and gold.
"What a fight, Jack! Oh, what a rally!
"So I'll tell you where Talbot's gone: It's Easter Valley."

CHAPTER 16

Who benefits?

On the way over the rainbow back to H-Town, I mull the question around in my head. Who benefits from Pop's kidnapping? Many have their reasons, including the Old Man and Samhain.

The Old Man would have free reign at the Pole. And the more stygian of Samhain's crew would be able to roam at all hours anywhere they wished in the eternal night of Christmas Eve. But I've plowed those snow drifts before and neither seems to fill the Christmas stocking. The costs seem to outweigh the benefits.

Elf unions aside, Pop is the reason the Pole, the Old Man's cash cow, exists in the first place. Without Pop, there is no Christmas. Without Christmas, sooner or later, there is no North Pole. It's in the Old Man's best interest to see that Pop stays in place and on task. What good is it to be the ruler of an abandoned wasteland, after all?

Samhain and his crew are in a similar position. Who cares about running free under the moon for eternity if your clientele, namely trick-or-treating children, are not awake to keep the business going?

Pretty soon, you and your ghouls would be forgotten about all together. And for Holiday folk, being forgotten by the humans is to cease to exist.

I've seen it happen.

Ever heard of Eye of Ra Day?

Exactly!

That's the reason Holiday Town, a city for beings who are

supposedly immortal, has a cemetery.

Anyway, so neither the Old Man or Samhain are to blame. But there is a connection with the October Country. Talbot's involvement is proof enough of that.

Based on the rap sheet I had Fred pull, Talbot doesn't have the brains or the jingle bells to pull off something on this scale.

And let's not forget, he was waiting for me in Necropolis. Someone tipped him off that I was coming—someone who had to have overheard my conversation with Dee back at City Hall.

Someone who benefits!

Without a snowflake of a doubt, before I take Talbot in, he and I are going to sit down for our own little heart-to-heart.

I reach H-Town and, out of habit, stop at a pay-palantir to call Mom. I freeze in mid-dial, realizing what a fruitcake I am. The feds will surely have Mom's line tapped.

Poor Mom. She's worried about her husband and now, with me on the run from the law, her son to boot. She must be doing horrible. It kills me not to be able to call her to let her know I'm alright, but that's how it is.

No point in trying to call and update Dee, either. With the ruckus back in Loveland, it's simply not safe anymore.

Heck, it never was.

I walk the back roads of H-Town until I reach the corner of Fifth and Bunny Trail. I make a right on the ol' hippity-hoppity-highway and before long, instead of pavement beneath my feet, it's gravel.

Soon, I'm out of the city all together, heading down the forest path that leads to Easter Valley.

The woods give way and the open, rolling fields of Easter Valley reveal themselves. Even at night, Easter Valley is a fine place to be, if a bit warm for my liking.

The flowers and trees are *very* alive and sway in time to the singing of night birds and the blinking of fireflies.

It's a happy scene.

You'd never know that just beneath Easter Valley's surface, the Burrows run long and deep, full of huge, nasty, anthropomorphic bunnies who'd just as soon thump you to pieces as look at you.

Yeah, I know what you're thinking. Easter bunnies are full of goodness and sharing. And that's true enough.

Velveteen, Hazel, and the others might run things up here—and even just below. But go down in the Burrows far enough and you enter the sewers—*metaphorically speaking*—that are Cottontail territory. And it's there that I must go.

I cross the field before me, looking for an entrance to the Burrows.

I am not disappointed.

I find a hole large enough to accommodate my size—or Talbot's for that matter, which is a good thing since I'm following his trail—and head down inside.

It's not long before the light from above peters out, so I take out the piece of borealis to guide me. I step over protruding roots and scurrying bugs, spiraling deeper and deeper into the earth.

I begin to wonder if I've entered an old, deserted network when I hear voices up ahead. I extinguish the borealis and proceed toward the sound, hoping the glamour will be enough to pass me off as a Cottontail.

I reach a bend in the tunnel and see light flickering from the other side. I peek around and see two bunnies, obviously Cottontails, arguing heatedly among themselves.

Though these aren't the first Easter Bunnies I've ever seen, I'm still amazed at the size of them. No garden variety rabbits are these! Each stands the full height of a Christmas elf from hind paw to ear tip. Their hand-like forepaws hold torches made of thin vines woven into tight bulbs. Light shines from the fireflies captured inside.

"I've been on watch for six hours!" the first bunny, a sour-faced rabbit with a chewed ear, says. "It's your turn to take over!"

"Just because I happened to be passing by," the second bunny, a rabbit sporting an eye patch, says, "doesn't mean I'm your relief. I've got other orders! Maybe he's your relief?"

I straighten where I stand, startled to realize the patch-eyed rabbit is referring to me.

So much for hiding.

At least the glamour's working. They seem to think I'm another Cottontail.

"Is that right?" Chewed Ear asks. "Are you taking watch?"

"I, er," I say coming out from around the bend, "that is to say—" Suddenly the tunnel begins to shake, dirt and dust falling upon our heads, with what sounds like the beating of a thousand drums.

"Assembly!" Eye Patch shouts and scampers down the tunnel in the direction opposite of me.

"But! But!" Chewed Ear pleads.

"Assembly," I say shrugging my shoulders. I chase after Eye Patch down the tunnel. I hear Chewed Ear cursing and kicking at the tunnel floor behind us.

I follow Eye Patch into an enormous rabbit-dug cavern already filled with hundreds of Cottontails. They push, shove, and argue amongst themselves, jockeying for a position close to the elevated platform of earth located at the cavern's far side.

For my part, I settle into a hopefully inconspicuous position along the herd's edge.

A fight breaks out between two of the largest rabbits in the cavern over who gets to stand nearest the pedestal. The smaller bunnies around them are knocked senseless in the wake of their battle.

I begin to wonder how much damage they will do before it's over when the biggest rabbit I've ever seen comes bounding through the herd and thumps both of them into unconsciousness with a mere flick of his hind paws. He leaps to the top of the platform and a name whispered in reverent fear passes through the herd—*Bugsy.*

He raises a forepaw and the cavern falls into total silence.

"Before I speak of the reason as to why I've called assembly," he says, "let us again remember our dear, fallen general, whose mantle I reluctantly assume, though I am unworthy."

The herd stamps its hind paws repeatedly upon the ground as a single unit and the cavern shakes.

Bugsy raises his forepaw again and the stamping stops.

"The herd above all else!" Bugsy says.

"The heard above all else!" the rabbits echo, their voices thunder.

"Loyalty to the herd!" Bugsy says.

"Loyalty to the herd!" the rabbits repeat.

"But what if I told you, my loyal Cottontails, that there is an impostor among us?"

The cavern erupts in shouts of outrage.

I gulp at my position along the herd's edge.

"What should the herd do with such vermin?" Bugsy asks.

The bunnies scream unrepeatable things. I begin to back away from the crowd for a nearby tunnel. I can't find Talbot if I'm pounded into an ice slushy by hundreds of rabbit paws.

"What if I told you, my Cottontails," Bugsy continues, his voice taking on a razor's edge, "that we know who the impostor is?"

I turn and bolt for the tunnel only to be greeted by four scowling rabbits. I try to shove by them but succeed only in being beaten down to the ground. Then numerous rabbit feet eclipse my vision and everything goes black.

Who benefits from Santa Claus's kidnapping?
Around the answer, Jack's mind was quickly wrapping.
Talbot was the muscle, but the brains were at City Hall.
It was someone who had overheard Dee's and his phone call.

Deep in the earth below Easter Valley,
The Burrows ran like twisting back alleys.
A notorious gang, there did dwell,
Big, bad, Easter bunnies, the Cottontails.

Jack ventured inside, hoping the glamour would stick.
He needed to stay disguised to pull off this trick.
The Cottontail gang, he needed to infiltrate,
And find the werewolf before it was too late!

He joined the bunnies in their assembly hall.
Bugsy their leader was the meanest of all.
He stood high on a pedestal and addressed the herd.
"There's an intruder among us! That is my word!"

Jack spun on his heels and tried to run out.
But the bunnies grabbed him and his head they did clout!
They stomped him up and down without uttering a peep,
Until darkness overtook him and he went to sleep.

CHAPTER 17

I am dreaming. I'm just a boy, back in the tropical rain forest, abandoned to thaw by the Old Man and scared to death of doing so when I hear the wonderful sound of sleigh bells ringing. It means the man who will become my father is here to rescue me in more ways than one—in every way that matters.

Then I'm strolling arm-in-arm with Dee along the Loveland shore on the day we first kissed. I lean in to do so, closing my eyes. When I open them to see if she's doing the same, it's not Dee before me but a snarling werewolf!

I awake from my dreams with a start, rising up and banging my head on the low roof of the burrow in which I'm imprisoned. I can't tell if it hurts or not. My body already feels like one giant bruise from my thumping at the hands and feet of the Cottontails.

"I was beginning to wonder if they'd killed you."

I turn and see a familiar man whose face I can't quite place sitting beside me. "Who are you?" I ask.

"You know perfectly well who I am," he says.

"No, I'm afraid—" in two shakes of a snow globe, Talbot changes into his wolf form and then just as quickly changes back.

"See now?" He asks.

I tackle him in response and pin him to the ground. I raise a fist to strike him and he begins to laugh.

"To be such a cool character, you're quite the hothead, Frost," he snorts.

"Where is my father?" I demand. "Where is Santa Claus?"

He finds this hilarious. "You wouldn't believe me if I told you!"

"Try me."

"It wouldn't make any difference, Frost. There's nothing you can do about it. We've both been played like drums. And now several hundred bunnies are about to make sure we both go the way of the dodo because of our stupidity!"

I look around the burrow, noting the logs jammed in the entrance—our prison bars.

"I can get us out of here."

"Who are you kidding, Frost? You think your glamour is going to save you? The Cottontails smelled you, an outsider, the moment you entered the Burrows. Besides, the magic's gone now. I saw them wash it off you—-though the water did freeze when it hit your skin."

I cross my arms. "Tell you what: If I get us out of here, you tell me where Santa Claus is the moment we're topside. Then you let me take you in. I can get the feds to go easy on you."

He chuckles.

"What are you laughing at, furball?" I ask. "Face it. Turning yourself in is your best option. You're running out of places to hide."

"You really have no idea who you're dealing with, do you?" he asks, still chuckling. "Okay. Okay. Get us to the surface and I'll tell you where the fat man is. Then we can worry about the rest."

"Deal."

I rise to a crouch and put my hand to my mouth, adjusting my fingers so that I can get just the right pitch. Then I blow.

"What was that?" Talbot asks.

"A whistle," I say.

"I didn't hear anything."

"You might have in your werewolf form. Besides, it wasn't meant for you."

"Oh, yeah? Who was it—?"

There's the sound of fierce scraping from the other side of the earthen wall at Talbot's back and then it collapses on top of him, covering him in dirt. A glaze-eyed mole on size with the Cottontails pops its head in through the hole created in the wake of the fallen wall.

"You called?"

"Hermie," I say, "I've never been so glad to see anyone in my life!"

"Pardon me if I can't say the same," the mole jokes, referring to its blindness. "How are you, Jack? Who's the wolf I smell with you?"

"I've been better, pal. This skuzzbucket of a werewolf is Larry. We need you to dig us out of here. We've got to get to H-Town, pronto."

"Certainly! Glad to help. Follow me."

Hermie turns in the hole and begins to dig at an incredible rate of speed. I lift Talbot, dirt covering and all, and shove him into the hole ahead me so I can keep an eye on him.

Hermie tunnels through the ground for what seems like hours, Talbot and me following at his heels. Suddenly he stops and sits up on his hind paws.

"Hermie?" I ask.

"Uh," he says, apprehension in his voice, "I think I should've taken that left turn at Albuquerque!"

The floor gives way beneath our feet and we go tumbling downward through the air. I look down and, with surprise, I see I'm about to land directly on top of Bugsy where he's perched amid the herd for assembly.

He's just as shocked.

I land on him and we go tumbling off the pedestal into the herd. Talbot and Hermie crash directly beside us.

Somehow, I'm able to get an arm around Bugsy's neck before he can recover from the fall.

"Freeze," I yell at the heard, "or your boss is a popsicle!"

The Cottontails start to creep forward. "Tell them to back off!" I say.

"You must be joking?" Bugsy replies.

I squeeze him tighter.

"Do I look like a clown to you?"

"Halt!" Bugsy screams.

"Wise decision. Now tell them to allow us passage."

"But—!"

I tighten my grip yet again.

"Allow them passage!" Bugsy shouts.

"All the way to the surface."

"All the way to the surface!"

Reluctantly, the rabbits move aside. We back slowly through them and enter the exit tunnels. We walk until we reach a turn that I recognize.

"Think you can get away on your own from here, Hermie?"

I don't have to ask the mole twice. I turn and see his hind-end disappear down a freshly dug tunnel.

"Well, uh, thanks—"

"Don't mention it," Hermie's voice echoes back down the tunnel.

I square my jaw and form two blocks of ice around Bugsy's hind paws so he can't follow. He cries out in surprise and outrage.

"You'll never get away with this, Frost." He says, his voice trembling with anger and cold, "I'll make sure of it!"

"Yeah, yeah. Take a number."

I grab Talbot by his arm.

"Come on. Let's go."

Moments later, we exit the tunnel through which I came in. Fresh air never smelled so good! But I don't allow myself time to savor it. I turn and, without saying a word, imprison Talbot's left foot in a block of ice.

"Hey!" he shouts. "That's cold!"

"Where's Pop?"

"Really, Frost! We just faced down the Cottontails together. I thought you and I were *pack* now!"

"We're not pack! We had a deal—I get you to the surface, you tell me where Pop is. Now, talk!"

"Alright! Alright! I'll tell you where you're precious jolly fat man is! He's—"

Talbot's eyes roll back in his head and he collapses to the ground to reveal a troop of feds firing sleep spells at me from the ends of their wands.

"Nutcrackers!"

I turn to run. Before I can go dim, I feel a spell connect between my shoulder blades. The last thing I see is the ground rushing up to meet my face.

Jack Frost awoke in a cell with his old enemy.
"Talbot!" Jack said, "You've been no friend to me!
"Where is Santa Claus? Tell me right now!"
"Take it easy," Talbot said. "Don't have a cow!"

"Now listen, Talbot," Jack said, "I'm not playing!
"Take me to my pop or your prayers you'll be saying!"
"Haha," Talbot laughed, "You're such a loon.
"I've been played for a sap, and you for a buffoon!"

"When we escape," Jack said, "you'll sing a new song.
"I've had things under control all along!"
"I don't see," Talbot said, "how we can get out.
"No matter how loud and how much you scream and shout."

"I've got my ways," Jack said with a wink.
"I come through in a clutch, perform best on the brink!"
"If you get us topside," Talbot said, "I'll go quietly.
"They've been keeping me here daily and nightly!"

The two of them escaped with the help of a mole.
They tunneled to the surface. Such was their goal.
But before Jack could take Talbot on to jail,
They were both put to sleep by the zap of a spell!

CHAPTER 18

I awake from another nightmare, the leftover echo of Pop's pleading screams in my ears.

I'm in jail.

Again.

Talbot beside me.

Again.

"Talbot," I say as I sit up on the cell's lone piece of furniture, a bench.

He ignores me and just rocks back and forth where he sits, a glazed look in his eyes.

"Talbot!" I demand.

Finally, he looks at me.

"I can count to ten!" he says with unbound glee. "One. Two. Apple. Ten!"

"Uh," I say, "I think you skipped a few there, pal."

"There was an unfortunate mishap during Mr. Talbot's interrogation."

I turn and see Father Time standing in front of our cell, Romeo and Jasmine, healthy and whole, at his side.

"It appears the Guardsman conducting the questioning used an improper spell. Rest assured he will be reprimanded. However, not to worry. Mr. Talbot should be right as rain in a millennium or two."

Father Time turns his attention from Talbot to me.

"We're hoping you'll come clean, son. And spare us all the potential for any further accidents."

"What are you talking about?" I ask, bewildered.

"Please, son. Don't play coy. Just tell us where your father is so we can go get him and get things back to normal."

I jump to my feet.

"You think I kidnapped Santa Claus?"

"The need for subterfuge has passed, Jack," Father Time says. "Before things went awry in Talbot's interrogation, he confessed you and he were in on this together from the beginning.

"He told us how you played the loving son all these years merely so you could one day usurp Santa's place of power. When you saw that day wasn't going to come fast enough, you took matters into your own hands.

"I guess the cube doesn't fall far from the iceberg."

"Liar!"

I leap at him, reaching between the cell bars to grab his robes. A few quick stunner zaps from Jasmine and Romeo knock me to the floor.

I lie there, *knowing*.

I curse myself for being so stupid and not putting it all together sooner.

Father Time turns to his officers. "Shut the door."

Romeo complies and closes the door to the room, shutting the five of us off from any eyes and ears that might be pass outside in the hallway.

I rise into a sitting position, still trying to fight off the pain from the stunners.

"Why are you doing this?" I ask. "What have you done with Santa?"

Father Time squats, using his staff as a prop, so that he faces me at eye level.

"If you're so smart, Jack," he whispers as he smiles, "you tell me!"

I look at him and shake my head.

"Your wife. Your son. How could you do this to your own son?"

"Quit babbling, boy!" Father Time says. "If you've got something to say, spit it out!

"Please, entertain us. Show us those supposedly great powers of deductive reasoning you're so famous for."

I sigh, wishing I had some eggnog to drink or a peppermint stick to gnaw on.

"Who benefits?" I say. "Who benefits from all this? That's the question you always have to ask."

I look Father Time dead in the eye.

"The answer is, *you.*"

"You wanted people to believe this was all about Santa, didn't you? You wanted us to believe that the November folk, in their unbound jealousy, kidnapped Santa Claus to stop Christmas and put Thanksgiving at the top of the holiday list.

"But that's only the smallest part of it, isn't it? Santa's kidnapping is just a convenient smokescreen that both accomplishes and hides your real objective."

"I'm impressed!" Father Time says, smiling mischievously. "Please, do go on."

"You enlist Old Man Winter's help to cover the kidnapping—ask him to brew a up blizzard that will cover the real perps' tracks—Talbot for one.

"But I'm guessing these two thugs here at your side also, considering you're letting them listen in on all this."

I point at Talbot. "Take a look guys. This is what happens to those who serve your boss!"

Jasmine and Romeo take a step toward the cell but Father Time calls them off. He's enjoying this little *explain all.* He wants someone to appreciate how clever he is.

What a Grinch!

"I guess it was the promise of a cut of H-Town business that got the Old Man to agree to help you. Income from the capital city would more than make up for any losses he might suffer from Santa's absence at the Pole."

Father Time nods. "Very perceptive of you!"

"It would have been easy enough for your boys to get their hands on turkey feathers to toss around the crime scene for the frame up. Of course, everyone would immediately assume it was Frankie the Gobbler. He's been the most vocal of the Thanksgiving bosses in his contempt of Christmas."

"Really, Jack," Father Time nods, "You do astound me! So much so, one has to ask why would I want to call in such a bright boy as yourself on the case?"

"Are you kidding me?" I ask. "As you said way back, my rep's well known. And with my own father being the one kidnapped, it would've looked odd—*suspicious even*—if you hadn't asked for my help."

Father Time grins, but it doesn't reach his eyes.

"Of course, of course. Nothing slips by you!"

"Talbot's assassination attempt on you was staged, as well. Like with bringing me in on the case, it was all an elaborate ploy to further cast suspicion away from you and onto the Gobbler and his crew. Romeo's attempt at capturing Talbot just made the whole thing all the more believable."

Father Time's grin fades into a scowl.

"But then, enter the bright and shining knight of ice crystal!"

"Yeah, exactly," I say. "What you didn't count on was my going after Talbot, much less coming back with evidence. He was supposed to make a clean get away."

"Touché!" Father Time says, his tone mocking.

"I guess you've got City Hall and the area around it bugged. That's how you overheard me say I was going to the October Country.

"You must have immediately gotten word to Talbot so that he and his pack could lie in wait for me.

"You probably reached him through Samhain, the being who hooked you up with Talbot in the first place.

"Like Old Man Winter, I guess you also lured the Halloween crime boss into this caper with the promise of a piece of the H-Town underworld."

"That's certainly one way to skin a cat," Father Time says, "Or, in this case, melt an ice man!"

"Your plan stalled again when the Count gave me Talbot's name. You didn't factor in one of Samhain's lieutenants having ambitions beyond those his master allows him, much less making a move on them."

"So that's how you found out who Larry was!" Father Time exclaims.

"Yep. But I should've figured out it was you behind all this before then, back in the October County, when Talbot and his boys jumped me."

Father Time leans in, genuinely interested.

"How so?"

"Let me back up a second.

"First of all, realizing that the crime scene was staged, that was a no-brainer. That Old Man Winter and Samhain had a hand in this, well, that was obvious too. But I couldn't wrap my head around why.

"I should've realized it was for the only reason that either of them do anything—*profit*. Then I should've asked myself who in the Holiday worlds could've supplied them with enough income to risk their regular cash cows. That should've immediately led me to finger you, the man with all the wealth of H-Town under his thumb."

"Good points all," Father Time says. "But I don't understand. What do any of them have to do with Talbot's October Country ambush being your tip off?"

"Like I said, Talbot was there waiting on me.

"He knew.

"Someone—someone who had to be at City Hall—tipped him off. With all other roads already leading to you, that should've been the star on the Christmas tree."

"All this impressive deduction," Father Time says, "but you still haven't answered the million dollar question, boy: why?

"Why did I do all this? Why did I kidnap Santa Claus?"

I slowly rise to my feet. Father Time rises to his own so that we're once again face to face.

"Because, you Grinch, the same reason your kind do anything. To gain power. *And to keep it.*

"Your one year of glory—of being mayor of the holiday worlds—it just wasn't enough for you. You couldn't bear the thought of Baby New Year's arrival.

"Unlike your dignified forefathers, the years before you, you didn't want to give up the throne and *pass on*. You wanted to be Father Time for all eternity!"

"And what's so wrong with that?" Father Time screams.

He loses his cool, shoving his underlings out of his way so

he can pace angrily around the room. Finally he comes back to face me.

"What's so wrong with wanting to live a little longer? To enjoy a little more of life?"

"Nothing," I say, "for anyone else but you. You have power over time—of your year and all those that came before you. That is near absolute power. It is a blessing. But for any one being to wield it longer than your kind do is wrong."

For all it's worth, I give Father Time the Eye.

"You waited until Santa Claus had cast the spell of eternal night. Then you kidnapped him to make sure he could never deliver Christmas presents to the boys and girls of the human world and undo the spell.

"You did this so that no more days would pass, ensuring your position as Father Time forever, with no thought of the cost to your family or the known worlds.

"In this act of ultimate selfishness, you've corrupted the natural course of things and brought shame to all the Father Times who came before you!"

"Silence!" Father Time screams.

He lowers his staff and, well, I *freeze*—freeze in time that is. Like an ice sculpture.

After a moment, Father Time seems to gather himself. His grin and happy demeanor return.

"I know you can hear me, Frost. And I say to you, *Bravo!*"

He does a prim golf clap on my behalf.

"For the most part, your logic has brought you to the heart of things.

"Yes! I had Santa Claus kidnapped. Yes! It was to ensure he could never deliver Christmas presents to the boys and girls of the human world and undo the spell of eternal night.

"And, lastly, yes, it was all to prevent the birth of my son, Baby New Year, and keep myself in power for all eternity!

"There! You have my confession in full—for all the good it will do you.

"You really should have considered my offer to take the heat."

"It wouldn't have brought Pop back. Something would've

conveniently happened to me in lock up before I made any contrived statement about his whereabouts."

"Astute as always." Father Time turns to Jasmine. "Prepare the mind-wipe spell."

Jasmine and Romeo turn to each other. Twin streams of ominous, silvery mist begin to snake out of their wands and weave in the air.

My frosty heart hammers in my chest. I've got to get out of here. I've got to break free of Father Time's spell. I've got to find Pop and stop this madman!

"Oh!" Father Time says as he uses his free hand to steady his staff. "Why Jack, you are the strong one, aren't you, my boy! I feel you struggling against my time-dampening spell. Do you have something you'd like to say before your IQ drops to that of a brick?

Suddenly, I feel his spell's hold on my mouth disappear. Unfortunately, it remains very much intact over the rest of my body.

"What have you done with my father?" I demand.

"Yes," Father Time says as he strokes his beard in consideration.

He turns to Jasmine and Romeo.

"Belay the spell. I've got a much better idea for Mr. Frost, here."

Father Time returns his attention to me.

"Good news, Jack, old boy! I've decided to let you see your father." Father Time's mirthless grin spreads wide across his face. "And I promise you, *it will be the last thing you ever see!*"

Father Time gestures to Romeo. "Zap him with a sleeper."

"No wait—!" I yell. But it's too late. Romeo raises his wand and the all-too-familiar blackness covers my field of vision.

Jack found himself in an H-Town jail.
"Just like old times. Yeah, just real swell!"
The wolf was beside him, drool hanging from his chin.
"Snap out of it, Talbot! Trouble we're both in!"

"I'm afraid," Father Time said, "there's been a mistake.
"The interrogation spell was more than he could take.
"Why don't you fess up, Jack? Why don't you come clean?
"We know you're the perp, working from behind the scenes."

In that moment, Jack Frost's cold heart fell.
He knew what his subconscious had been trying to tell.
The answer had always been there, circling in his mind.
"You kidnapped Santa Claus! It was you, Father Time!"

Father Time turned to his guards and said, "Shut the door.
"Such a bright boy, Jack. Please, tell me more!
"Talbot, Old Man Winter, they were all a smokescreen.
"From the beginning, it was you who was the fiend!"

"You kidnapped Santa Claus to stop time and halt the hour,
"It was the one way for you to always stay in power!"
"Brilliant!" the mayor said. "Too bad we have to stop.
"It's high time I showed you where I'm keeping your pop!"

CHAPTER 19

"Jack."

I know I'm dreaming again when I hear Pop's voice.

"Jack, wake up, son."

It's so hot in the dream. Like a sauna. It's agonizing.

"Jack, it's me, your father. Wake up, son!"

I feel my body being shaken. My eyes flutter open and the large, dark silhouette of a man stands over me, the blazing sun forming a corona around him.

"Pop?" I ask. My voice sounds terrible—as brittle as a frozen twig.

"Quick, son. Let's get you into the shade."

Pop lifts me and carries me under the canopy of a nearby tree. Santa wipes the water of my melting scalp from my eyes and I see that he has stripped down to only his boots and underclothes.

He's filthy. His silvery hair and beard are full and unkempt. He's also quite a few pounds lighter than when I last saw him.

"You've lost weight," I say, my voice a whisper.

"And you will, too, unless we get you out of here soon." He hugs me to his chest. "Oh, son! It is so good to see you."

"Where are we?" I ask. "How can the sun be out when it's still Christmas Eve?"

"It's still Christmas Eve in the time you came from. If I had to guess, I'd say we're currently sometime around the end of the Cretaceous Period. It's where Father Time and his cronies dumped me, *and now you*, for safe keeping."

I think about the elevator in City Hall, the one that runs from the big bang up to present day, and realize exactly how Pop and I got here.

"Oh, son, you wouldn't believe the things I've had to endure!"

"You and me both—"

Pop gestures for me to fall silent. I do so and try to listen. But it's too hard. Too hard to do anything but lie here.

Great Ak, it's hot!

Pop perks up beside me.

"Pop, what is—?"

Again, I fall silent at his urging. Then I feel it. The ground shaking beneath our feet every few seconds. The tremors are small, but growing steadily. They remind me of the Cottontail's thumping, only magnified a hundred fold!

"We've got to get out of here!" Pop says.

He jerks me to my feet and throws my arm over his shoulder. He trots deeper into the rain forest surrounding us, more or less dragging me along. We pass around trees, deadfall, and bubbling pits of what will one day millennia hence be petroleum.

"What, Pop? What's the—?"

I see the gigantic head of a tyrannosaurus rex drop below the forest canopy to sniff the ground. Pop dives behind a fallen tree, pulling me along with him.

"Okay, son," he whispers. "He only smells me. You're just water as far as he's concerned. I'll run to the left and draw him away from you."

"No way, Pop!" I whisper.

"It's not open to discussion, son."

"If you take off, I'm going to yell at the top of my lungs to make sure he has a thirst quencher in me before he gets you as the main course."

"You wouldn't!"

I struggle to do it, but I grin back at him. It's answer enough.

Pop scowls, looking as mean as a jolly fat Santa Claus can, which isn't very much.

"It's only a matter of time before the dinosaur finds us. What are we going to do?"

"We'll beat him to the punch. Look, I've got an idea. See if you can get us back to one of those tar pits we passed."

He nods and lifts me to my feet. We both glance back at the

T-Rex. It's still sniffing the ground, but closer now.

Too close.

We stumble along, circling back in the direction we came, the T-Rex doing likewise. At last, we reach a clearing overflowing with bubbling pits of goo.

"There," I say, nodding to a large pit on our right. "That one looks big enough. Take us over—"

My words are drowned out in the tooth-rattling roar of the T-Rex. We look back and see the dinosaur crashing through the forest toward us, its enormous, razor-sharp jaws spread wide.

"He's spotted us!" I say. "Quick, get us to the other side!"

Pop moves as fast as I've ever seen. In seconds flat, we reach the opposite side of the pit.

"Lower me down!" I plead. "Hurry!"

I stretch my hand out above the tar pit, reaching out to the tiny droplets of moisture hanging in the air. Pop realizes what I'm doing and protests.

"No, son! You're too weak! It will kill you!"

I ignore him and concentrate, praying I can do this before the T-Rex gets close enough to be spooked by it. A thin sheet of ice forms beneath my hand and begins to snake out over the pit.

"Come on!" I say.

The T-Rex grows larger and larger within my field of vision.

"You can do this! Come on!"

The dinosaur's roar thunders in my ears.

The ice finishes covering the entire pit just as the T-Rex bursts through into the clearing. I collapse, rolling over onto my back so that I see an up-side-down version of the beast as it gallops toward us. It dodges around several pits and I begin to worry my plan won't work.

"Come on, you big, stupid thing, come on!"

I shouldn't have worried. Instead of noticing the ice cover and slowing down, the T-Rex charges straight for us. The ice cracks with its first step and the dinosaur tumbles face-first into the bubbling ooze.

"Yeah!" I shout.

I slam my fist on the ground in triumph as the T-Rex sinks below the surface. I turn, exuberant, to face Pop. My smile drops when I see the tears rolling down his rosy cheeks.

"He was going to eat us, Pop," I say.

"I know," he says wiping his face. "I know. But he was just an animal, doing what he was born to do. He didn't know any better."

"Yeah, I guess you're—" Agony shoots through my body.

I look down and see I'm only an ice shaving of my normal frosty self. That last little stunt with the ice cover did me in.

I'm melting.

Fast!

Pop takes me in his arms.

"If only I had a little bit of the Pole here—a little bit of home grown magic. I could get us out of here lickity-split."

I try to speak, but my mouth is only able to form a single world. "Pocket."

Pop nods. He releases me and reaches into my cloak pocket. A smile lights up his bearded face along with the bit of aurora borealis as he pulls it out.

"If it's one thing I know," Pop says as he lays a finger to the side of his nose with his free hand, "It's how to make an exit!"

I hear the ding of an elevator and then a rectangular hole opens in space before us. On the other side is the box-shaped interior of the City Hall time-evator.

He drags me inside.

"What floor?" He asks.

A smug grin covers my face.

"There," I say, pointing to one of the buttons, "the last Ice Age!"

Jack woke up and opened his eyes to see,
He was with Santa Claus back in prehistory.
"Pop, it's good to see you, but it's so darn hot!"
"Jack, we're stuck here," Santa said. "Such is our lot."

"Where is here, exactly?" Jack asked. "Melting is my ice."
"The age of the dinosaurs. And they aren't very nice!
"Let's get you in the shade, before you melt away.
"Somehow we've got to get you back home to present day!"

At that moment, a roar through the forest rang.
Then out from between the trees, a big T-Rex sprang!
"Let's get the holly out of here! Come on, Pop, run!
"If that T-Rex catches us, you and I are done!"

Jack and Santa bolted, but much to their dismay,
There was nowhere to run, no path for getaway.
"I'll freeze a tar pit, Pop, and let the T-Rex crash in."
"No way, son! You're weak. The act would mean your end!"

Jack froze the pit anyway, having little choice.
When the T-Rex broke through, to cheers they gave voice!
Then using a little magic leftover from Pole side,
Santa called the time-evator to give them both a ride.

CHAPTER 20

Great Ak, am I *frosted*!

If Fred were here, I guess he'd use video game terminology and say I was *powered up*, or *leveled up*, or whatever. That little trip into the Ice Age was just the thing to put the ice back in my freezer!

But, poor Pop! He went from one extreme to the other—tropical heat to freezing cold. I look at him in the elevator beside me. His skin is, for him, an unhealthy blue, and his teeth are chattering.

"We've got to get you some proper clothes."

"I won't argue with you there!" he says through chattering teeth.

"Hmmm," I say, "Is there any way to get to a specific time and location? These buttons don't seem to pinpoint any time period smaller than a century."

"Yes, I've used this time-evator before," Pop says. "Just press the century you want and merely concentrate on the exact time and place. The time-evator will take care of the rest."

I press the button for the twentieth century and concentrate. The time-evator dings and the doors open to the bustling Thirty-fourth Street of mid-century Manhattan.

"Ho-ho-ho!" Santa laughs, his voice full of approval. "Macy's department store, circa nineteen-forty-seven. Good call, son!"

"Wait here," I say, "I don't think anyone needs to see Santa Claus running around New York in his underwear."

"Agreed."

I go dim and exit the time-evator. I cross the street and enter Macy's. It's packed with humans shopping for Christmas presents. Holiday lights and decorations are everywhere and the music of Christmas carols floats softly through the air. I slip away from the masses to search the hidden areas behind the individual shops.

At last, I find what I'm looking for—a locker room with a Santa Claus costume hanging on every hook. I pick one out that looks like it would fit Pop and stuff it under my trench cloak. Then I head back toward the elevator.

I reach the street and see a small child in old, worn clothes staring at me, her mouth agape.

Sometimes, kids, the ones with pure hearts and pure eyes, can see me even when I'm dim.

There's a woman—I'm guessing the child's mother—rummaging in a trash can behind her. It melts even my cold heart. I walk over to the child, her eyes growing wider with every step I take. I put my finger to my lips, gesturing for her to be quiet.

I squat down in front of her and gesture for her to wait a moment. I take out the borealis from my cloak and the little girl gasps as it illuminates her face. I place it in her hands and then form a sparkling ice chain that I attach to it. The magic of the borealis should be enough to keep it intact permanently.

"From Santa," I whisper, giving her a wink. She places the chain over her head and slips it around her neck. She cradles the borealis in her hands and then looks up at me, her tiny face full of love and gratitude. Without warning, she throws her arms around my neck and squeezes me in a tight hug. After a moment, I hug her back. I use my magic over cold to banish it from this child. Hugging me will be the last time she ever knows Winter's harsh, bitter touch.

We separate and I motion for her to put the borealis down the front of her shirt.

"Secret and safe." I whisper.

She gives an exaggerated nod of understanding.

"Merry Christmas," she whispers.

"Merry Christmas," I say as I rise.

I turn and walk back to the time-evator without giving the child another glance.

In the end, Frost is what Frost is, after all.

Pop is ecstatic to see the clothes I brought him and immediately starts putting them on.

"Good job, son! These are just about like those your mother sews for...Jack? Are you crying son?"

"Something was in my eye," I say as I wipe away a frozen tear. "Let's go."

Pop presses the button for present day and we rocket up toward Father Time's office. I make myself forget about the little girl and concentrate on what I plan to do when I get my hands on ol' FT!

"Easy, son," Pop says. "Save it, now."

I glance around and see that there's frost forming on the walls.

"He's going down, Pop! For what he's done, he's going down!"

The door opens to Father Time's office and every clock in the room goes off in alarm. Three feds I've never seen before are there waiting on us. They raise their wands and fire.

But I'm ready for them!

I throw up a shield of reflective ice and the spells go bouncing around the room. One even strikes its caster and he falls to the ground, stunned.

A quick wave of my hand and a blizzard-cold wind gallops across the room, freezing the other two feds where they stand.

I skate over the ice lain across the floor in the wake of my wind and grab the stunned fed by his sash, pulling his face up to mine.

"Where's Father Time?" I demand.

He struggles unsuccessfully to speak. At last, he manages to raise an arm and point to the large crystal ball mounted on the wall among the clocks. Father Time is on it giving a press conference, Jasmine, Romeo, and Dee at his side.

"...Unfortunately," Father Time's image says from the TV, "Talbot's accomplice, Jack Frost, met his end during an escape attempt."

"The holly I did!" I shout. "Come on, Pop. We've got to get down there!"

We jog to the time-evator and go inside. I press the button

for present day and concentrate on the lobby. The press room is also on the ground floor. We reach the lobby and then bolt into the press room just as Father Time announces his regret that it doesn't appear there's any chance of finding Santa Claus.

"I beg to differ!" Santa bellows.

Every head in the room turns and voices his name in surprise at seeing him. Cameras flash and he's bombarded with a hundred questions. He ignores them all and shouts over the crowd.

"Father Time, you've been very naughty!"

"This man is an impostor!" Father Time shouts. "He's with a known felon! Seize them!"

Jasmine and Romeo spring into the air. The crowd shrieks as they dive-bomb us. A wave of my hand sends them falling to the ground like the heavy blocks of ice that they now are.

Pop and I press our way forward through the crowd.

"It's Father Time who is the criminal here!" I shout. "It was he who actually kidnapped Santa! Father Time said Santa was lost, but he was holding my pop hostage the whole time! Everything else is lies, just like him saying I was dead!"

"It this true?" the reporters Father Time ask in a hundred different variations. "How do you explain this?"

Pop and I press onward to the stage.

"He didn't want to give up being Father Time. And the only way he could stay in office was to make sure Baby New Year never arrived! That's why he needed to keep Santa from delivering presents. He wanted time to stand still! He wanted it to be Christmas Eve forever!"

The reporters bombard Father Time with questions until he loses it.

"Silence!" he screams as he waves his staff in a broad arc.

I erect a protective ice shield around Pop and myself just in time to prevent the time-dampening spell from washing over us. The rest of the crowd is not so lucky. They go as still as the victims in Old Man Winter's palace, frozen in time.

Father Time grabs Dee by the neck and pulls her to him.

"Don't follow," he shouts, "or your little friend gets it!"

He ducks out of the room, dragging Dee along with him.

"Pop," I say, "he's got Dee!"

"I think I can lift this spell off these good folks, son. You go on. Get him! I'll catch up."

I nod and run out of the room after Father Time.

After a quick stop at the last Ice Age,
Jack Frost was poised and ready to take center stage.
But his pop Santa Claus needed an outfit.
So back into the past is where Jack Frost went.

Jack slipped into Macy's Department store,
Grabbed a Santa outfit and headed out the back door.
Out in the alley, a little girl saw through his disguise,
Although Jack is hidden from human eyes.

He gave her piece of magic light on an ice chain,
Jack Frost's loss was the little girl's gain.
He wished her Merry Christmas and bid her goodnight,
Then went back to Holiday Town to make things right.

He burst into Father's office, ready to rock.
The Holiday Guards, he froze in an ice block!
"Look, Jack," Santa said. "Father Time is on the news."
"Move! To the press room! Not a moment to lose!"

The mayor was there, acting all haughty.
"Father Time," Santa said, "You've been very naughty!"
With Dees as his hostage, Father Time ran.
"Quick, Jack!" Santa said. "You must stop that man!"

CHAPTER 21

I reach the lobby just in time to see the time-evator doors closing with Father Time and Dee inside. The mayor hurls a spell with his staff just as the doors shut and I drop to the floor, allowing the charm to pass harmlessly over my head.

I run to the time-evator. I curse as I watch the lights over the time-evator door descend in number. Father Time is taking Dee to the basement level. At least he's not hopping around in time. There's that to be thankful for!

I press the call button on the other time-evator but nothing happens.

"Jammed! Nutcrackers!"

I look around the room, searching for a stairwell. I spot a door in the corner and scramble over to it and fling it open.

Bingo!

I don't waste time with the stairs. I simply form an ice chute that spirals down over them. I hop on and slide to the bottom where I burst through the doors and into the basement.

"Dee!" I shout. She's lying against the wall cradling her neck and ankle.

I rush over to her and kneel at her side.

"Can you walk?"

"No. I twisted my ankle when he tossed me out of the time-evator. That's why he left me behind."

"When I get my hands on that lowlife—!"

"Don't worry about me, Jack. I'll be fine."

She points to a tunnel on our right.

"He went that way!"

I linger for only a second, caressing her chin between my

thumb and forefinger. Then I rise to my feet and take off after Father Time. I don't bother going dim. The magic of Father Time's staff is too powerful for my clothes to hide me from him.

I run through a maze of tunnels filled with steaming pipes and fire hoses. I duck around a corner and dive just in time to dodge a spell from the end of Father Time's staff. I hear him curse but when I pop up to return fire, he's gone.

I proceed down the tunnel with caution. He almost had me with that little ambush. I've got to turn this game of cat and mouse around, somehow.

I exit the tunnel to enter a large, underground loading dock. It's filled with boxes, crates, and forklifts—any of which could serve as his hiding place.

What can I do to draw him out? I ask myself.

And then I answer myself just as quickly.

His Ego!

I recall how he enjoyed my recounting the events of his plan to remain Father Time—how he *wanted* me to know—how he wanted to have his Machiavellian workings admired.

Yes, it's a man with an ego who thinks himself worthy enough to wield absolute power for all eternity!

I slip behind a skid of shrink-wrapped boxes.

"Hey, FT!" I call from my hiding place. "I've got to hand it to you, when you screw up a plan, you do it big time!"

I fall silent, listening for a response. I hear nothing. I crouch and duck-walk forward to another hiding place behind a row of boxes.

"And right on inter-holiday news, too! Man I bet every man, woman, and child in the holiday worlds are laughing their buns off at you right—!"

I hear zapping spells streak across the room. They strike the boxes serving as my hiding place and send them scattering.

I duck and roll behind a forklift, dodging oncoming spells. A few more blasts hit the forklift before all falls silent again.

"That was a close ice shave," I whisper.

If nothing else, I've learned he's within striking distance. If he can hit me, then I can hit him! I've got to press him. Get him fuming mad and careless.

"That the best you can do?" I shout. "I think you need your eyes checked. You missed me by a mile!"

I wait.

Nothing.

"But that's to be expected from a Father Time whose year has passed. You must be ancient by now! A real old codger way past his prime who's too senile to realize when he needs to give up the reins!"

"Shut up!" Father Time screams.

I pop up from behind the forklift, knowing he will be doing the same to try to get a shot at me.

I pray I'll be faster.

I am.

But not fast enough.

My shot goes over his head as he ducks behind a stack of wooden pallets. It hits the wall behind him where it spreads out in a large patch of ice.

"Peek-a-boo, I see you," I whisper.

I count on him keeping still for a moment and crawl forward to another hiding place behind a large barrel on his left flank.

"It must be rough to see all your hard work and planning slip through your fingers," I say. "And to think, you were the very one to call in the guy who would bring it all crumbling down around you. Namely me!"

I get ready to wait out his fire and volley back, but no spells ever come. Inspiration strikes and I form an ice sculpture of myself. Just enough of its stocking-fedora is sticking out from behind the barrel to make the old man think it's me still crouched behind it.

I crawl out from behind the barrels on my belly and inch my way to a position behind the dispatch desk.

"Yes, one of us was just a little bit smarter than the other," I say throwing my voice at my ice-double. Like the whistling, it's another little trick I've picked up along the centuries.

"Well, let's be honest here. One of us is smart, and the other is just plain stupid—the one who has delusions of grandeur and multi-world domination, that is. Not that I'm naming any names!"

I crawl out from behind the desk to a stack of pallets a mere ten feet to the left of Father Time's hiding place. Almost home. Just got to get him angry enough to pop out again.

"What would you do with eternity anyway?" I ask, again throwing my voice. "It's not like you have the brain capacity to do anything—!"

"Shut up!" he screams as he pops out from behind his hiding place.

I freeze him solid just as he lowers his staff to shoot. I sigh in relief and get up from my hiding place and walk over to him.

You can imagine my surprise as I round the stack of pallets and see another Father Time crouched there, his staff raised to fire. It does and this time, it's me who freezes!

Father Time rises to his feet. "Yes, one of us here is certainly stupid," he laughs. "And since it's not me, let me clear things up for you, Frost."

He taps the back of frozen Father Time's head with his fist.

"Look familiar?" he asks. "He should. He's me from three minutes ago—the *me* you made angry enough to come out of hiding.

"That was me before the near miss with your ice blast brought me to my senses. I realized I had to bait you. And using my staff's powers to bring this old boy into the present seemed like just the thing. Obviously, it was!"

Nutcrackers! My own trick used against me. What a snowflake I am!

"Oh, Jack my boy!" Father Time says, ecstatic.

He moves forward and seizes my shoulders.

"I'm almost sorry this has to end. This is the most fun I've had all year!"

He turns and paces as he talks. It must be something he does when he gets excited—or angry—like back in the H-Town jail.

"Now, I know what you're thinking, my boy, but don't you worry. As you pointed out, I am the master of this year and all those that came before mine. And contrary to what I said earlier, as you might have guessed by now, the time-evator works just fine!

"I'll just do a little time-traveling to the day this all began and make sure to smooth out the rough patches in my scheme you mentioned during our little talk earlier."

He stops and whirls to face me.

"But what about you? There's no guarantee you won't come back into the mix to foul things up again."

"Hmmm?"

Father Time strokes his beard and starts pacing again.

"Yes. What to do about you?"

A moment later he turns to face me again.

"I've got it! Oh, yes, my boy. This should be quite interesting. I've wondered about it before, but never quite dared to do it."

He rushes up to me and puts his face in mine.

"I've always been curious to see what would happen if I chronologically regressed a holiday person to the time before the humans—to the time before there was anyone around to give the forces and seasons of the world a name and a face!

"Would they explode, implode, or simply fade from existence? What's say you and I find out, shall we?"

Father Time's mirthless grin spreads wider than I've ever seen it.

"But I'm afraid, my boy, one way or another, it's the long, silent night for you!"

He lowers his staff and points it at me.

That staff.

It's the source of his powers. If only I could get it out of his hands.

The staff's tip begins to glow and Father Time's eyes grow wider and wider.

"Yes," he says excitedly, "Yes! I can feel the years coming off you! Century after Century!"

Father Time's nervous habit kicks in and he begins to rock back and forth on his feet.

If I'm going to get out of this and stop him, I've got to do it now, before I become less than a memory.

Unlike Old Man Winter, my powers are somewhat limited. He can freeze with a thought.

Me? I like to channel the cold through my body, especially my hands. It's not absolutely necessary, but it makes it a heck of a lot easier for me. But it's a hang-up that's almost cooked my Christmas goose here.

To beat Father Time, I've got to think outside the icebox. If I have to use my body to channel the magic, fine.

But that doesn't mean I have to use my hands!

"Closer, now!" Father Time says as he rocks excitedly. "Almost there!"

I send the cold snaking out from my feet across the ground. It forms a thin sheet of ice along the floor as it advances toward Father Time.

"Yes, yes!" Father Time is all but dancing now. "You're there at the dawn of civilization. You're little more than a flickering image now! Just the spark of an idea in some Cro-Magnon's—!"

The ice reaches Father Time's dancing feet and he slips. For a moment, he seems to hover in the air, his arms and legs flailing like those of a lumberjack trying to keep his balance on a rolling log.

Then gravity kicks in and he lands smack on his back, the wind rushing out of his lungs. His staff goes tumbling out of his hands across the room and immediately his spell over me is broken.

I don't give him time to recover.

I pounce on top of him, seizing his robes in my hands.

"You rotten, no good, liar!" I say, shaking him. "You were supposed to be our leader and you double-crossed us!"

I feel my anger rise within me and it brings the cold with it—the wild, uncaring blizzard that always rages in my heart—the storm that only wants to freeze and destroy!

"You kidnapped my father! Almost killed us both!"

The blizzard of my fury takes shape around us. In seconds, we're knee deep in snow, Father Time's clothes and beard frosted over.

"I should do the same to you! You'd deserve it! I should freeze you until you—!"

"Son."

It's Pop.

It's Santa Claus.

His voice is soft. I feel his hand come to rest on my shoulder.

"This is not the way, son. You're better than this."

I turn and shout in Pop's face.

"He tried to kill us! He tried to stop the birth of his own son. He wished that his own son never be born!"

I turn back to rage at Father Time.

"Do you know how that feels? Do you?"

I feel Pop's arms close around my shoulders.

"It's okay, son," he says. "It's okay. Poppa's here. Let him go, now. It's okay."

I shudder with anger and frustration.

And fear.

Fear of myself.

Then I abruptly release Father Time and bury my face in Pop's beard and chest.

Pop hugs me and lets me cry there until the storm, both inside and out, passes.

Then Pop helps me to my feet.

"Take his staff, son," Pop says. "Wait for me over there."

I nod and obey, picking up the staff and walking with it over to the loading dock entrance.

Pop lays his finger to the side of his nose and the color returns to Father Time's face. Pop helps him off the floor.

"Your year is long up, my friend," Santa Claus tells him. "You know that, don't you?"

Father Time starts to protest, but somehow, when he looks into Pop's eyes, all the anger drains out of him.

Father Time nods and begins to sob.

"I'm scared," he says, his voice small and sheepish.

"It's okay," Pop says as he places a hand on Father Time's shoulder. "New things are always scary, at first."

"I don't want to *end*," Father Time says.

"End? Why, there is no end. Only new beginnings, new states of being."

Pop places an arm around Father Time's shoulder and gestures to the air. A vision of a bright and shining future appears before them. It is not fairy magic, but the magic of truth.

It is the most beautiful thing I've ever seen!

"Just as the humans rise from and return to the fabric of the cosmos," Pop says, "so shall you return to the fabric of time. You shall join with your forefathers and go on and on to make up all the new years that come after you, forever and ever. This is not something to be feared, but embraced!"

Pop turns to Father Time and holds him at arms' length.

"Are you ready?"

The two men hug.

When they release each other, Father Time nods.

"Then go, my friend," Pop says. "Join with the past so that you may become tomorrow unending."

Father Time turns and walks into the vision of the future, his face alight with a brilliant smile.

Then he and the vision of the years to come are gone.

Out in the lobby, things had gone south.
"Downstairs, Jack!" Then Time's hand covered Dee's mouth.
"You won't catch me, Jack. Now or later!"
Then they disappeared into the time-evator.

Jack pressed the call button. "Nutcrackers! Jammed!"
Into the stairwell, his body he rammed.
Over the stairs, he formed an ice chute.
Then he skated down. Man, did he scoot!

Jack reached the sublevel to find Dee sitting there.
"He tossed me aside, Jack, taking little care."
"Tell me, Dee, which way did he go?"
"He went to the right. Be careful. Stay low!"

Jack found the mayor, and him he did seize.
"I'm sorry, Jack! Don't hurt me, please!"
But Jack wanted to freeze him, he was so mad.
"You kidnapped my, pop! You deserve it, you cad!"

But Santa Claus appeared and calmed Jack down.
"Don't stoop to his level, son. Don't be anger's clown."
"I'm scared," Father Time said. "I don't want to end."
"Your year is up," Santa said "Now a new one begins!"

EPILOGUE

"So you gave *half* of all that reward money to that little girl and her mother?" Dee asks in disbelief.

"Yep. Money well spent if you ask me."

"Well, what are you going to do with the rest of it?"

She leans across our park bench and tickles my chin, teasingly.

"You know how I like bright and shiny things!"

I smile at her. I know she's a creature of the night, but her beauty is especially stunning on sunny days like today.

Ha. Sunlight. Days.

I was beginning to wonder if I'd ever see either again! Thank Great Ak Santa's back at the Pole and time in full swing once again.

"Actually, I've been thinking about moving my office to H-Town."

"Here?" She gestures to the mostly deserted park we're seated in, but I get her meaning. "But you always complain about how hot it is. And you've got that pet polar bear cub now."

"Ha! He's hardly a cub anymore. That one grows like a Christmas tree. Anyway, with the reward money the city gave me for finding Pop, I can more than afford the cooling bill for both of us."

"That reminds me, you never told me—when did you realize Father Time was behind all this?"

"He claimed Talbot confessed that I was in on it with him. I knew that was bogus. It caused all the other clues that had been circling around in my head to fall into place.

"I guess it all worked out in the end."

"More or less. There is only one thing I couldn't figure out, Dee."

"What's that?" she asks as she snuggles against me.

"Why did you do it?"

Dee sits back up and looks at me in shock.

"Pardon?"

"Why did you convince Father Time to kidnap Pop?"

"Jack," Dee says, "if this is some kind of joke, it's not funny!"

"The only thing I can figure is, somewhere down the line after we split up, your ambitions for success got twisted into some kind of monstrous lust for power."

"Stop it, Jack. I said, this isn't funny!"

"Was it easy to seduce Father Time? To turn him away from his wife and unborn son?"

"I—I don't know what you're talking about!"

"I'm talking about how you always wanted to be a rung above everyone else on the political ladder.

"I'm talking about how you were the only one I told I was going to the October Country—the only one who could've phoned Talbot to let him know I was coming.

"I'm talking about why Talbot, a known felon and Halloweenian, would dare get involved in such a scheme behind Samhain's back."

"You think I brought Talbot into this?"

"Oh, I admit, for the longest, I assumed Talbot's part in this was Samhain's doing. But that wasn't right at all was it, Dee?

"You played Talbot just like you played Father Time.

"Just like you've played me from day one.

"Even at the end—your own kidnapping. That hurt ankle of yours. It was all an act. A set up so you could send me down the right tunnel for Father Time's ambush."

"This is ridiculous! I did no such thing! And I'd never heard of Talbot before in my life!"

"Oh no?" I say as I pull out the document Fred gave me. "This printout of his known associates reads different.

"Yeah, I had a little more time to look over the names toward the bottom of the list after everything settled down. Imagine my surprise to find yours there!"

Dee's shock turns to a scowl that turns into a self-satisfied smirk.

"Yes, Jack. You're right.

"*As always.*

"It was me. It was always me!

"I convinced Father Time to stop the new year. Do you think that fool could've ever come up a plan to make a grab for eternal power on his own?

"I've had you all eating out of my hand from the beginning!"

"Why Dee? Why did you do this?"

"Aren't you listening, Jack? Father Time was always a boob. He was nothing but a figurehead during his entire administration. I was calling the shots from day one!

"It was a trend I'd hoped to continue for all eternity. From behind the scenes, I was going to rule the holiday worlds beneath the shadow of everlasting night!"

Dee snarls at me.

"But you had to come along and mess things up!

"I told that old fool it was too risky to bring you into this, but he insisted it would look suspicious if we didn't.

"I could've figured out an excuse, but he wouldn't wait. He made me call you right away, the old windbag!"

"And I'm glad of it."

I rise to my feet.

"Well come on, Dee. Let's go."

"What?"

"I'm taking you in. Don't make this any harder than it has to be."

Dee laughs, the sound high and shrill.

"You're kidding, right? That printout is circumstantial at best. Talbot associated with a lot of folks who aren't criminals.

"Jack, my dear, you have no proof and I'm certainly not going to confess!"

I sigh.

"You already have, Dee."

Her face fills with alarm.

"What are you talking about?"

I open my cloak and shirt to reveal the wire I'm wearing.

"I told you before, Dee. You should be careful what you say. You never know who could be listening in."

Dee's jaw drops in stunned realization.

The feds I've had listening in exit their hiding places among the trees and walk toward us.

"I wouldn't try to run, sweetheart," I say, my voice grim.

I turn and begin to walk away in the opposite direction of the approaching feds.

"Jack—!"

"Goodbye, Delilah."

I hear the feds reach Dee and begin reading her her rights, but I don't bother looking back.

Father Time was right about one thing—it's going to be a long, silent night alone for yours truly.

Hoo-ray! Hoo-rah! Time was back in full swing.
Christmas was saved and now the New Year did ring!
Jack Frost saved the day. Now all was well.
But there was still one last piece of story to tell.

Jack and Dee sat on a bench in the H-Town park,
Laughing and talking, happy as a lark.
"I love this," Dee said. "We should do it another time."
"But tell me one thing, Dee: Why did you commit the crime?"

"What do you mean, Jack? This isn't funny!"
"Don't play coy, Dee. Was it power or money?
"Why did you have Father Time kidnap my pop?
"Confess, Dee. The final shoe, please drop."

"You're right, as usual, Jack. You always are.
"Without my brains, Father Time wouldn't have gotten far.
"He was a patsy. I ran things from behind the scenes.
"I'm wicked Halloweenian, Jack. It's just in my genes."

"I'm sorry to hear that," Jack said. "Let's be on our way.
"Don't make me laugh," Dee said. "I'm not going away.
"You don't have any evidence, facts, or proof!"
"I've recorded your confession, Dee. I'm a master sleuth!"

SECOND EPILOGUE

"Frost Detective Agency. Christy speaking—-just a moment." Christy puts the caller on hold just as I walk in the front door of my new office in H-Town. Why would I hire a witch as my administrative assistant after my dealings with Dee, you ask? What can I say? I have a soft spot for Halloweenians.

"Jack," it's the chief of the Holiday Guard. She says it's urgent."

"It always is. I say as I waltz by Christy's desk, dropping her lunch off in my wake. "Tell her I'll call her back in a minute."

"But Jack—!"

"In a minute, Christy!"

I saunter back to the room I've set up for Fred—-larger than my own so as to accommodate his equipment, *the little nutcracker*—and knock on his door.

"Open, it is," he calls from the other side. I open the door and find him at his computer, as usual.

"Heads up!" I say as I toss him his sandwich.

"Very much, thank you," he says.

"What kind of hip-hop lingo is that?" I ask.

"Hip-hop, so last decade is. Talk in Yoda-speak, now do I."

"Yoda-speak? Does this have anything to do with those movies you saw last week?"

"Greatest films ever, they were!"

I shake my head and leave Fred to his work.

I open the door to my office and a half ton of fur and muscle crashes into me.

"Down, boy!" I say as I scratch the polar bear's head.

I hand him a large fish I got from the H-Town market. He swallows it in a single gulp.

"Greatest films ever or not, I still don't know if I like the name Fred came up with for you, *Chewie*."

Chewie snorts and begins sniffing around in my bag.

"No, no! You've had your lunch. That's mine."

I sit and throw my feet up on my desk. I'm about to take a bite out of the snow cone I bought for my lunch when my globe rings.

Reluctantly, I pick it up.

"Christy, I told you—!"

"Frost?" It's not Christy's voice I hear, but that of the chief of police. "Frost, where have you been? No! Never mind that. Is your crystal ball on?"

"Why?"

"Just turn it on!"

"What's the big—?"

"Turn it on, Frost!"

I sigh and pick up the remote and pop on the idiot ball I have mounted on my office wall. The picture comes on to reveal someone in a mask standing in front of the familiar tanks of the H-Town magic works.

"—And I will release this toxin," the masked man's image says, "into the H-Town magic supply in exactly one hour if Detective Jack Frost does not present himself to me, alone and unarmed. This is not a hoax—"

"Frost," the chief's voice says over the phone. "Frost, are you there?"

"I'm on my way, chief!"

Without bothering to hang up the globe, I leap over my desk and skate out the door, knowing the city is depending on me.

"I'm on my way!"

And so our story ends on this last page.
We hope you enjoyed it and found it all the rage!
We hope we entertained you and on a journey took,
Your imagination while reading this book.

But now is the time for sleep, work, school, and play.
We'll always be here for you to visit on another day.
We hope you'll come back, should Jack Frost skate again.
There are more crimes to solve, more cases for Jack to win.

And so we bid you farewell, auf wiedersehen, goodbye.
Keep your head in the clouds, and the twinkle in your eye!
Stay young at heart and you'll always be all right.

Thank you for reading THE LONG SILENT NIGHT!

THE LONG SILENT NIGHT
CLASSROOM GUIDE

DISCUSSION QUESTIONS

1. The Long Silent Night: A Jack Frost Mystery is an unlikely combination of a traditional holiday tale and hardboiled detective fiction. What are some things you can name that, on the surface, wouldn't seem to go together but actually make for a great combination?

2. In telling the story of The Long Silent Night, Jack Frost uses a lot of Christmas-centric slang. A) What are some classroom-appropriate examples of slang you and your friends use in daily conversation? B) Why do you think people use slang in general?

3. Jack has two fathers--his biological father, Old Man Winter, and his adoptive father, Santa Claus. Do our genetics make us who and what we are, or is it our environment? Could it be a combination of these two factors and others? Please defend your answer.

4. The story of The Long Silent Night hinges upon a mystery. What is it about a mystery that appeals to so many people? What makes for a good mystery? Please explain your answer(s) in detail.

5. Classic Rankin-Bass Christmas cartoons and 1940s detective books/films inspired the author to write The Long Silent Night. What things inspire you (and why)?

6. Throughout The Long Silent Night, characters and places are often revealed to be at odds with the public's perception of them. For example, the seemingly cute and cuddly Cottontails of Easter Valley are actually criminals. What are some real world examples of people and/or places not being who and/or what they claim to be? Defend your answer.

7. In the first epilogue of the story, Jack Frost is forced to make a great personal sacrifice in order to see that justice is served. A) How do you think that made Jack feel? Why? B) In this instance, what might the author be trying to tell the reader about how life often works in general? Please explain your answer in detail.

MATCH THE VOCABULARY WORD

TO ITS CORRECT DEFINITION

Anthropomorphic___
Archetype___
Aurora borealis___
Benefactor___
Brogue___
Celestial___
Decrepit___
Epiphany___
Fedora___
Fisticuffs___
Kaleidoscopic___
Lackey___
Lycanthrope___
Machiavellian___
Nexus___
Sarcophagus___
Stygian___
Subterfuge___
Transient___
Wry___

DEFINITIONS

1. using or expressing dry, especially mocking, humor
2. having human characteristics
3. **impermanent; a person who is staying or working in a place
4. for only a short time
5. a primitive mental image inherited from the earliest humanancestors--a recurrent symbol or motif in mythology, art, or literature
6. deceit used in order to achieve one's goal
7. a person who gives money or other help to a person or cause
8. very dark; relating to the mythological Styx River.
9. a marked accent, especially Irish or Scottish, when speaking English
10. a stone coffin, typically adorned with a sculpture and/or inscription
11. positioned in or relating to the sky; extremely good.
12. a connection or a series of connections linking two or more things.
13. worn out or ruined because of age or neglect.
14. cunning, scheming, and unscrupulous
15. a manifestation of a divine being; a moment of sudden insight; a religious festival occurring January the Sixth.
16. a low, soft felt hat with a curled brim and the crown creased lengthwise.
17. a werewolf
18. fighting with fists
19. one who is subservient to another person or group of people—usually to an unhealthy, self-harmful degree
20. having complex patters of colors

FURTHER READING

The Life and Adventures of Santa Claus by L. Frank Baum
The *Encyclopedia Brown* series by Donald J. Sobol
A Christmas Carol by Charles Dickens
The Boogeyman by Shane Berryhill
Dragon Island by Shane Berryhill
The Adventures of Chance Fortune series by Shane Berryhill

ABOUT THE AUTHOR

Although Shane Berryhill is jolly, overweight, and gray bearded, he still contends he is in fact not Santa Claus. His books aimed at readers both young of age and young of heart include Chance Fortune and the Outlaws (an official selection of both the New York Public Library's Books for the Teen Age and the Texas Library Association Lone Star Reading list), *The Boogeyman, Dragon Island,* and others. Shane lives with his wife and son--and their pet puppy dog, Kwazii--in Chattanooga, Tennessee. Connect with Shane on Facebook at his "Shane Berryhill, Writer" page and on Instagram via "shaneberryhill1".

Curious about other Crossroad Press books?
Stop by our site:
http://store.crossroadpress.com
We offer quality writing
in digital, audio, and print formats.